THE RED WASTELAND

THE RED WASTELAND

A PERSONAL SELECTION OF WRITINGS ABOUT NATURE FOR YOUNG READERS

Edited by Bruce Brooks

Henry Holt and Company   New York

Henry Holt and Company, Inc., *Publishers since 1866*
115 West 18th Street, New York, New York 10011

Henry Holt is a registered
trademark of Henry Holt and Company, Inc.

Published in Canada by Fitzhenry & Whiteside Ltd.,
195 Allstate Parkway, Markham, Ontario L3R 4T8.

Library of Congress Cataloging-in-Publication Data
The red wasteland: a personal selection of writings about nature for
young readers / edited by Bruce Brooks.
p.   cm.
Summary: A compilation with commentary of essays, observations,
excerpts, and poems about nature by authors as diverse as J.-H.
Fabre, Rachel Carson, and Italo Calvino.
1. Nature—Literary collections.   [1. Nature—Literary
collections.]   I. Brooks, Bruce.
PZ5.R28   1998   [Fic]—dc21   97-42568

ISBN 0-8050-4495-7 / First Edition—1998
Designed by Meredith Baldwin
Printed in the United States of America on acid-free paper. ∞
10 9 8 7 6 5 4 3 2 1

For mockingbirds everywhere

CONTENTS

THE RED WASTELAND

PREFACE

It really is accurate to say, "Science is words."* And that's all it is. Science is not the growth of a virus in a petri dish filled with a carefully monitored solution of monkey blood and salt water at 36 degrees under blue light in a third-floor laboratory at the National Institutes of Health in Bethesda, Maryland. No. Science is what happens when the head honcho of that lab writes up a report on the growth of the virus under those particular conditions—an article describing, interpreting, analyzing, maybe even speculating about that growth—and then publishes it in a professional journal or in a book or reads it as a "paper" at an important international conference of other scientists, who are the only people in the world capable of grasping what he is going on about.

*I consider numbers to be just another kind of language—words free of spin.

Science is definitely not "nature." Nature is what happens all over the place, all the time, *all by itself,* whether we notice or not. The green magic we scientifically call photosynthesis is taking place in trillions of leaves on billions of trees and bushes from Alabama to Zanzibar every minute the sun is out, even if there are no people in white coats sitting around a laboratory somewhere discussing it—or a bunch of kids sitting, rather bored and restless, in science class half listening to a biology teacher spell out photosynthetic mechanics.

Ever since human beings started to write stories and observations in words, they have chosen both science and nature as constant subjects for their essays, poems, and books. This is because writers are moved by curiosity, and curiosity is moved by the unknown. Some of these people are "pure scientists" committed to the cycle of controlled experiment and observation and conclusion; some are nonscientific persons—we could call them "naturalists"—armed only with senses and curiosity, interested in telling about what they find around them in whatever language they find most accurate or convincing. Often, these two ways of studying the world blend together, at least a little; rare is the scientist who doesn't stand

back sometimes and just say "Wow!" without grabbing his test tubes, and rare is the naturalist who
doesn't try a little experiment with what he or she
finds, however inexpert the experimental technique
might be by today's scientific standards.

A lot of these people have been great writers, thank
goodness, driven to put their observations into words
for us to read. Even if you hate science class, it's nice
to have some things written down—for example, the
way a sea cucumber turns its intestines inside out and
dangles them at a predator in the hope that the display
of guts will ruin its appetite. How cool is that? And to
think we'd never know if someone hadn't watched it
and thought it was cool too—and then written about
it. What good does it do us if something really spooky
happens between three wolves meeting silently in an
Alaskan forest and the person who watches never
brings it to our attention?

Sometimes the drive to write about something as if
it is happening makes for very strange literature. In
this book, for example, is a story in which a woman
writes about what it was like looking into the eyes of
a hyena that was eating its way up her arm, swallowing
chunks of her flesh (there goes the bicep!) while, she
would have us believe, *she* was thinking coolly about

the special peristaltic gift hyenas possess of being able to swallow meat without relaxing the ferocious chewing of their locked jaws. Gee, isn't this interesting (oops, and there goes the tricep). . . .

The selections here have not been chosen because they relate the most important "discoveries" of science or because they exemplify the most poetic descriptions of sunsets over misty lakes or the delicate colorations of butterfly wings. Nor have these pieces been chosen to show different "writing styles." What I want to do is show not how people *write* about what happens in the natural world, but how they *think* about it.

Because as a writer, I must tell you: Behind every paragraph lurks an attitude. That's what's interesting, really, for us writers *and* us readers. In describing how a weaverbird makes its nest every spring, one writer can reveal that he thinks nature is holy and birds are our equals in importance and we shouldn't mess with them and the grasses they weave, while another writer can reveal his belief that man is the rightful master of the earth and ought to try copying those weaving techniques and making hats to sell at resorts even if it means swiping the grasses used by the birds and leaving them homeless and eventually dead, while another shows her feeling that the nest "means" nothing—it almost hasn't even happened—until someone has taken it into a laboratory and disassembled it and counted the strands used in its construction and analyzed where the bird probably picked up the nine different varieties of fiber it combined in the weaving. . . .

Many of us cannot resist the urge to know stuff we didn't know before, to understand it a little, or at least to watch. It drives some people nuts that nature is "going on" out there while we are sitting around not being aware of it. Some entomologists (insect scientists) speculate that there are probably 100,000 species of beetle alive all over the world that they have not even discovered yet. Maybe there's a white beetle shaped like a snowflake that sneaks around Antarctica living off penguin poop. Maybe there's a two-foot-long black night beetle that sneaks onto ships docked in Amsterdam and kills rats hiding in the hulls. Maybe there's a radioactive beetle that eats uranium and, if found and put to use, could replace X-ray machines or atomic bombs or cathode-ray tubes or something.

And what about secret things that might be happening down there where the oceans are seven miles deep and no human has ever gone?

Fortunately, when a human *does* go there, or an entomologist does capture the snowflake beetle on some penguin excreta, he or she is almost certain to write about it. Then we'll have it, nice and safe and slightly contained, in words. We may learn something that saves our lives, or that is merely intriguing to find out about. Keep reading. You never know what someone might write about.

"THE BAT"

BY THEODORE ROETHKE

Sometimes, one cannot help suspecting that writers will do anything at all to set up a killer exit line. Such, almost, is the case here; Roethke's shocking act of abrupt personification must be one of the best. Isn't it interesting that what is scary here—what grabs us and gives that little What-happened-to-gravity? twist—has nothing to do with the critter, whom we have been with since the beginning of the poem, but, rather, with the presence of the kind of face that ought to be most comfy and familiar to us? This "integration" of man with Nature—as represented by a beast—exemplifies a scary, absurd resolution to the question nearly every writer in this book will ask: Where does Man fit? Where do I?

By day the bat is cousin to the mouse.
He likes the attic of an aging house.

His fingers make a hat about his head.
His pulse beat is so slow we think him dead.

He loops in crazy figures half the night
Among the trees that face the corner light.

But when he brushes up against a screen,
We are afraid of what our eyes have seen:

For something is amiss or out of place
When mice with wings can wear a human face.

GREEN LAURELS: THE LIVES OF THE GREAT NATURALISTS

BY D. C. PEATTIE

This piece shows that nature writers themselves become a kind of hybrid—as if a "naturalist" were only part human, with the remainder composed of a unique insight into or "belonging" to the world of animals, plants, wind, water, and all the mysteries we can only glimpse when these "hybrids" serve as our intermediaries and interpreters. The man who put this book together actually gets a bit pompous and snotty about certain naturalists or scientists who didn't make his final cut; at times, despite his fine words in the passage included here, which is drawn entirely from the foreword, he can be found looking down his nose at this or that person whose theories or writings or personal unimportance kept him or her out of the book. But even if Mr. Peattie doesn't always live up to the statements expressed here, he obviously believes in them. And he puts them into words very nicely.

We must remember from time to time that the people whose words we are reading have themselves read a great deal about the creatures or plants or places they describe for us. With a few exceptions, perhaps, these writers did not just find themselves face-to-face with a Galapagos tortoise or a polyphemus moth by coincidence; these people were interested in nature already—they were students and watchers and notetakers, far from inexperienced in thinking about how things happen in the world. It doesn't matter whether it was greed, literary hopes, or a personal contrariness toward "big ideas" and an urge to blow theory away by firsthand witnessing. We readers don't need to care about why these writers got curious. It is enough that they all fell prey, utterly, to that curiosity. And a writer driven by the particular inspiration of intense curiosity is a writer who is most likely to put down words that are carefully chosen, passionately representative, deeply felt—and thus worth reading, no matter how well they have been "proved" or "disproved" by the progressive march of science since. As Mr. Peattie points out, these people who thought hard, watched carefully, and wrote well deserve our fullest respect and enjoyment. After all, the science writers we most revere today may themselves find their "facts" overthrown by the ideas and "facts" of tomorrow. Doesn't matter. Let's read them anyway.

Of all things under the sun that a man may love, the living world he loves most purely. In a lifetime's devotion to it there is no self-interest. Men so devoted tell us of their well-companioned days, but they are reticent about their best reward. In Nature nothing is insignificant, nothing ignoble, nothing sinful, nothing repetitious. All the music is great music, all the lines have meaning.

So from these men we should receive at least a reflection of the immense reality they behold. Theirs are the eyes that understand what we all see. They sketch in the great *systema naturae*, and we the gapers peer over their shoulders. And, since we are invisible to them, we take a glance at the profiles of the men themselves, stand off to see them in perspective against the background of their times, or come close to notice wrinkle and peccadillo.

I am writing about the naturalists, distinguished— as well as they can be—from the biologists. These latter I think of as the indoor men, the naturalists as the outdoor men. To put it another way, the naturalists deal with living beings *in situ*—in their active, vital inter-relations; the biologists are more concerned with isolated organisms, living under controlled laboratory conditions, or they may be interested solely in the activity of one organ, or even with partially inorganic matter, chemicals and the physics of protoplasm. . . . In so vast a subject a writer must choose his province, and mine lies out of doors, where all is alive and various.

Its reigning figures flock to the mind. To give account of them only would be to create the false impression that a few naturalists have stood out in solitary grandeur, owing nothing to others, owed all by humble disciples. To do justice to all would be to write little less or more than a biographical dictionary of the subject. I wish that such a volume existed; to my great inconvenience, I have found none such, or even a good history of natural history in any language that I can read.

So I have chosen rather to write of the mighty names, with abundant reference to many others, both the quasi-great and the big little men. The task of selection and exclusion has been a poignant one. That I have no space to characterize all who come into the story, the reader must forgive, and he will believe, I trust, that I am not unaware how far the lesser men have built up the great ones.

With regret I have omitted the great Nature writers and those men of letters who have appreciated Nature but brought nothing new to science. W. H. Hudson's nostalgic recollections of the wild life of the pampas, his tender feeling for the English countryside, can find no place in a short account of the progress of natural history. Maeterlinck and Richard Jefferies too belong to the literature of Nature. Our own American Thoreau was no scientist; he took many an occasion to deride and deplore science, and so on his own pleading we must applaud him rather in his chosen role of Transcendental moralist and poet of Nature. If Thoreau cannot be admitted to these pages, still less may his follower Burroughs.

Nor do I suppose that all the figures here discussed at some length are equally important. John Bartram was by no means such a great naturalist as Camerarius, who comes in for little more than honorable mention, and Rafinesque's genius is debatable in the extreme compared with that of Huxley whom I admit only in connection with his fight for evolution. But my endeavor is to represent many branches of natural history, especially those dear to me, and I emphasize typical men of each age. I am human enough, moreover, to dwell upon the more piquant personalities. We love, alas, not so much for virtue as for charm. . . .

For there is a story to be told greater than that of any great life. This is the story of man facing his world—man in his nakedness, abstract curiosity glittering in his simian pupils as he stares at the wall of the primeval wood and listens to its sounds, and wonders. The distinguishing characteristic of the human species is our ability to put two and two together and get the abstraction, four. We correlate, we deduce, and thereby we create something. The creation of art is a familiar idea, but science too is a creation. It is not Nature itself, it is what we make of Nature, an arrangement, a pattern, an interpretation.

Scientists believe that in the making of this pattern there is a gradual perfection. In art there appears to be no progress; who dares say that sculpture today has advanced beyond Scopas? In art there is only change; science, which traces its beginnings back to that identical moment when art began—the charging bison on the cave walls in Spain—is conscious of growth.

So confident of progress is science that in our tri-

umphs lurks the danger that we will think too poorly
of the eras which held views no longer ours. But the
history of science will correct such juvenile vanity.
The old ideas are the ancestors of our own; we build
upon the sunken piers of obsolete wisdom.

I have spoken of my selection of certain individuals to stand forth and tell the greater story of how
Nature has unfolded in the mind of man, and I have
given, perhaps, the idea that whim has guided me in
the choosing. But indeed they come cast for these
rôles, and when I omit such a splendid scientist as
Louis Agassiz, for whose story I have the greatest
personal fondness, it is because most of what he stood
for in natural history had already been expressed
by Cuvier, the master of the school of nineteenth
century anatomy.

So, more than life-stories of men, these are biogra-
phies of ideas. And beyond and above that, they
are—what I suppose I cannot help writing—incidents
from the adventure of Nature itself. I have been trying to see what men so much greater, if more ignorant,
than your modern, were looking at. I have been trying
to retrace the way into a world marvelously the same
as that about us today, and yet new and fresh and

strange because man had not yet explained it to himself. That explanation is but partially completed; we do not know what tenets cherished today must be discarded tomorrow. Forever the challenging whistle, the bright flash of truth, eludes us in the green growing forest.

BIRDS, BEASTS, AND MEN: A HUMANIST HISTORY OF ZOOLOGY

BY H. R. HAYS

This excerpt, relating the eccentricities of the great Roman philosopher Pliny, is part of Hays's attempt to track the progress of the study of animal life (and the life around animals) from ancient times onward through various revelations and revolutions about what science was, where its boundaries lay, how it fit (or fought) with religion or myth, whether it could be based on speculation about invisible things or must be limited to that which has been observed, etc. Like many drawn to the mysteries of nature, Pliny sounded pretty ingenious—and pretty peculiar. But doesn't Pliny represent most of us far better than does the grandly educated scientist? He wanted to discover a nature he could live within, not one he could only understand from the outside.

Myth had operated on the basis of fantasy, association, or analogy. Since thunderbolts were like hurled weapons, it was stated that someone with the name Zeus threw them from the sky. But as we know, scientists were eventually to discover they could manufacture miniature thunderbolts in the laboratory without the aid of the ruler of Olympus.

The scientific type of mind, therefore, is inclined to rule out the supernatural when it cannot be substantiated by fact. In the sixth century, however, it was a bold breakthrough for Xenophanes, a disciple of Anaximander, to point out: "If horses or oxen had hands and could draw or make statues, horses would represent the forms of gods like horses, oxen like oxen." Freedom from superstition of this sort is absolutely necessary for rigorous scientific thinking. Once it is attained, instead of staring at diseased livers in order to prophesy the outcome of battles, men attempt to study the function of the liver as a part of the digestive system. Instead of observing the flight of birds in order to decide whether the gods are pleased or not, men attempt to identify the birds and study their migrations. And as regards our own science, instead of placing imaginary zodiacal animals in the sky, men take a look at real animals and work out a system of classification.

As it happened, those who followed the Ionians were not of the same temperament. The mixture of poetry and magic called religion continued to possess political power for many centuries. It sometimes hindered and never helped the progress of science.

This does not mean that myth and poetry do not shed profound beauty on human life—as long as they are understood as myth and poetry and not taken literally or used for the wrong reasons by priests and politicians. . . .

Basically a sturdy rationalist, Pliny sometimes makes us feel that he collected many of his oddments and fables simply because he wanted to show the extreme credulity of humanity. And perhaps he, too, even as the modern reader, found them rather entertaining.

Yet he certainly, with a straight face, created a kind of anthropology of the absurd: men with dogs' heads who conversed by barking, men with one leg apiece who got about hopping, men with eyes in their chests, men with no mouths who drank through a straw inserted in their nostrils. Most of these wonders were said to occur in India and Ethiopia, but the climax came when he announced: "Upon the coast of Africa are the Ptonebari and the Ptoemphani, who have a dog for their king, and him they obey according to the signs which he makes by moving the parts of his body, which they take to be his commandments and they religiously observe them."

In less fantastic moments Pliny could list recipes for cooking, give a good account of Greek painting, sound agricultural advice, an exhaustive description of the gold mining industry and textile manufacture, then suddenly swing into a diatribe against the Roman mania for statues in which he tells us that they set up statues of Marius Gratidianus in every street and knocked them all down again when Sulla came to power.

As a zoologist he was not an experimentalist and he does not seem to have practiced anatomical research. His method, as we have already noted, was to cite authorities he had read (two thousand books he tells us). If he seldom made a choice between fabulous and more sober statements, he often cited his authorities, leaving the reader to judge if they were to be believed. All his authors were listed in Book I. In general he followed Aristotle but with less scientific organization. He lumped together the land animals, the birds, the sea animals, and the insects, and cataloged each group in terms of its habits. He followed this with a rundown of anatomy that was basically Aristotelian. We are obliged therefore to appreciate him for his amusing fantasy and also more or less as a naturalist who wrote at times rather lyrically about nature.

Examples of his contribution to the folklore of zoology abound in his study of the elephant. He made perfectly sound remarks about elephant training, but mixed in with these observations were such statements that certain snakes are avid of elephant blood. "They submerge themselves in rivers and when the pachyderms drink, coil 'round their trunks and bite them inside the ear. These snakes are so large that they can contain the whole of an elephant's blood, and thus they drink their prey dry at which time the elephant collapses in a heap and the intoxicated serpents are crushed and also die."

Of lions he tells the Androcles story, although he attributed the adventures to one Mentor of Syracuse. From the fabulist Ctesias he cited not only the manticore but also the yale, an animal with movable horns which could be pointed forward and backward. The basilisk also appears in his pages, although he described it merely as a twelve-inch-long snake with a diadem of bright markings on its head. It killed bushes with its touch, scorched grass, burned rocks, and when speared, its lethal power could run up the spear and kill the huntsman. Another story, which was to be repeated many times, was that of the offspring of the bear, shapeless little lumps of flesh, which had to be "licked into shape" by the mother.

India, that hotbed of miracles, produced turtles with shells so large they could be used to roof houses. Indeed charming was the behavior of the small parasitic crab which lives in the fan-mussel. When the shellfish opened, it presented its dark side to tiny fishes. These darted in and filled up the vacant space. The crab, having watched carefully, gave the body of the shellfish a gentle nip. The shell closed at once, killing the fish upon which it fed, leaving a share for the cooperating crab.

The Plinian version of the phoenix must be cited, for it differs somewhat from later fables. According to Pliny, it lived 540 years, then constructed its nest of wild cinnamon and frankincense, and lay on it until it died. From its bones and marrow a sort of grub was born which grew into a child, who celebrated the funeral rites of its parent by carrying the nest to the city of the sun near Panchaia and placing it on an altar.

He was critical enough, however, to reject the story of the death song of the swan.

When it came to the nightingale, Pliny wrote with enthusiasm. He tells us: "The sound is given out with modulations, and now is drawn into a long note with one continuous breath, now varied by managing the breath, now made staccato by checking it, or linked together by prolonging it, or carried on by holding it back; or it is suddenly lowered, and at times sinks to a mere murmur, loud, low, bass, treble, with trills, with long notes, modulated when this seems good—soprano, mezzo, baritone; and briefly all the devices in that tiny throat which human science has created."

Let us listen to Pliny the ecologist in a statement which has greater implications now than in his time. He defended the earth, saying:

It is true she has brought forth poisons—but who discovered them except man? Birds of the air and wild beasts are content merely to avoid them and know well enough how to watch out for them. . . . It is true that even animals know how to prepare their weapons to inflict injury, yet which of them, except man, dips its weapons in poison? As for us, we even poison arrows and we add to the destructive power of iron itself. It is not unusual for us to poison rivers and the very elements of which the world is made, even the air itself, in which all things live, we corrupt till it injures and destroys.

This sound and prophetic statement balances a good deal of Pliny's spinning of tall tales.

As a conscientious observer of nature, when dealing with things he knew, he could be exact:

Some people think that butterflies are the most reliable sign of spring, on account of the extremely delicate nature of that insect but in the year in which I am writing, it has been noticed that three flights of them were killed one after another by the cold weather and that migrating birds arriving on January 27 brought hope of spring that was soon dashed to the ground by a spell of very severe weather.

One of his most attractive pieces of writing is his discussion of stars in the heaven and insects in the grass which, he maintained, appear at the same time:

Nature not only assembles a troop of stars, the pleiades, but she has made other stars in the earth to show him the true seasons. It is as though she cried aloud: why gaze upon the heavens, plowman? Why search among the stars for signs? The nights are shorter now and the slumber your weary work imposes upon you is less. Behold I scatter here and there among the weeds and grass, and display in the evening, special stars when you unyoke and cease from your day's work. I cause you to marvel and gaze upon this wonder, so that you shall not pass them by. Do you see how these fireflies screen their brilliance, which resembles sparks of fire, when they close their wings and how they carry daylight with them even in the night?

Pliny's death has often been cited as a proof of his interest in science. At the end of his life he had been made an admiral and given the command of a fleet at Misenum, an ancient town in the Bay of Naples. In August, A.D. 79, his sister pointed out a cloud of unusual size and appearance. Pliny was just out of his bath. He climbed a hill and was greeted with an eruption in the shape of a pine tree, which he was later to discover came from Mount Vesuvius. At first, he ordered a light vessel to take him to the scene so that he might observe the phenomenon, but then, hearing that people in nearby villas were in danger, he ordered out a large galley and steered for the coast near Vesuvius. Cinders and blackened pumice stones fell on the deck, but he disembarked at another town which commanded a full view of Vesuvius. Although his friends were alarmed, Pliny calmly took one of his innumerable baths. People were abandoning the villas near the mountain which blazed and shook the earth with violent concussions. Pliny passed a dreadful night amid showers of stone but in the morning went down to the beach to observe the eruption. At this time he was already corpulent and suffering from asthma. He was lying down on a sail when a new outburst of fire and smoke dispersed all his attendants. Apparently the thick sulfurous vapor obstructed his breathing, and at this point he died. Three days later, when the eruption had abated, his body was found, his nephew wrote, "Fully clothed as in life; its posture was that of a sleeping rather than a dead man."

This was the end of Rome's most industrious natural philosopher. His work sums up what was known and believed at the end of the classical world.

THE GOSHAWK

BY T. H. WHITE

*The uncomfortable arrogance of making a wild animal
into a pet is something that doesn't occur to most people
who do it. People tend to "love" their pets eventually,
and usually feel that this benevolence is about all an animal ought to expect—it's more than it would get in the
woods and rocks, right? Not many people who take care
of animals—buying them food, shots, even sterilization
surgery, all at no cost whatsoever to the animal!—feel like
anything but animal* lovers. *And they are, at least as far
as the individual creatures under their care. The larger
question of how that animal, as both a captive and a
potentially free wild thing, might fit into nature is rarely
considered. Once again, where does Man fit? Where do
his rights stop, and the animal's begin?*

*T. H. White decided to buy himself a young goshawk
to train, and he never really got over this question. When
one reads his small book, which mixes intricate details of*

his hawk's growth and progress in learning how to obey White with a rough history of falconry (in which humans use a predatory bird to do a little hunting for them) and his personal reflections on what this strange creature really is, one cannot help but feel that this guy is not a born falconer. He cannot stop admiring the bird for the innate wildness that frustrates his (rather halfhearted) falconer's trials, and he cannot stop pointing out how weird and repressive this stuff must be for this otherwise free-flying lord of the skies. Most of all, he cannot stop falling in love with this bird and the larger wildness of nature it belongs to.

All of this may be seen in the passages from chapter one that are included here. But White's indecisiveness is not all we get, and is certainly not what makes this book a cult classic. The fact is, White can flat write beautifully. Whether he is describing a feather pattern, a moral misgiving, or a speculation about his bird's life without him, he gives it to us precisely, in fascinating, compact prose. There is probably more reading pleasure in this ninety-page book, including the troubled philosophical stuff, than in most simpler, longer nature memoirs. When the goshawk escapes at the end, we regret it more than White does—because we know it means he won't have anything

*to keep writing about. But maybe he'll get a pet alligator
next and try to train it. . . .*

Tuesday

When I first saw him he was a round thing like a
clothes basket covered with sacking. But he was
tumultuous and frightening, repulsive in the same way
as snakes are frightening to people who do not know
them, or dangerous as the sudden movement of a toad
by the doorstep when one goes out at night with a
lantern into the dew. The sacking had been sewn with
string, and he was bumping against it from underneath: bump, bump, bump, incessantly, with more
than a hint of lunacy. The basket pulsed like a big
heart in fever. It gave out weird cries of protest, hys-
terical, terrified, but furious and authoritative. It
would have eaten anybody alive.

Imagine what his life had been till then. When he
was an infant, still unable to fly and untidy with bits
of fluff, still that kind of mottled, motive, and gaping
toad which confronts us when we look into birds'
nests in May: when, moreover, he was a citizen of
Germany, so far away: a glaring man had come to his

mother's nest with a basket like this one, and had stuffed him in. He had never seen a human being, never been confined in such a box, which smelled of darkness and manufacture and the stink of man. It must have been like death—the thing which we can never know beforehand—as, with clumsy talons groping for an unnatural foothold, his fledgeling consciousness was hunched and bundled in the oblong, alien surroundingness. The guttural voices, the unbirdlike den he was taken to, the scaly hands which bound him, the second basket, the smell and noise of the motor car, the unbearable, measured clamour of the aircraft which bounced those skidding talons on the untrustworthy woven floor all the way to England: heat, fear, noise, hunger, the reverse of nature: with these to stomach, terrified, but still nobly and madly defiant, the eyas goshawk had arrived at my small cottage in his accursed basket—a wild and adolescent creature whose father and mother in eagles' nests had fed him with bloody meat still quivering with life, a foreigner from far black pine slopes, where a bundle of precipitous sticks and some white droppings, with a few bones and feathers splashed over the tree foot, had been to him the ancestral heritage. He was born to fly, sloping sideways, free among the verdure of

that Teutonic upland, to murder with his fierce feet
and to consume with that curved Persian beak, who
now hopped up and down in the clothes basket with
a kind of imperious precocity, the impatience of a
spoiled but noble heir-apparent to the Holy Roman
Empire. . . .

Night

The yellowish breast-feathers—Naples yellow—were
streaked downward with long, arrow-shaped hackles
of burnt umber: his talons, like scimitars, clutched the
leather glove on which he stood with a convulsive
grip: for an instant he stared upon me with a mad
marigold or dandelion eye, all his plumage flat to the
body and his head crouched like a snake's in fear or
hatred, then bated wildly from the fist.

Bated. . . . It was a word that had been used since
falcons were first flown in England, since England was
first a country, therefore. It meant the headlong dive
of rage and terror, by which a leashed hawk leaps from
the fist in a wild bid for freedom, and hangs upside
down by his jesses in a flurry of pinions like a chick-
en being decapitated, revolving, struggling, in danger
of damaging his primaries.

It was the falconer's duty to lift the hawk back to the fist with his other hand in gentleness and patience, only to have him bate again, once, twice, twenty, fifty times, all night—in the shadowy, midnight barn, by the light of the second-hand paraffin lamp.

Birds I Have Known

BY ARTHUR H. BEAVEY

Yeah, well, it's the ones you haven't *known—and there are millions—that are the lucky ones.*

Compare the arrogant God-told-me-humans-are-the-masters tone of this nineteenth-century "gentleman"— who got to know birds only by keeping them as pets (Moses, a kestrel, was such a pet)—with the personal humility and respect for animals exemplified by Hudson, Fabre, and half a dozen of the other writers in this book. You won't find T. H. White getting cranky at his bird because it dares to strike at its "master" with its talons, and you won't find any of these authors disposing of a class of birds as "failures" because they didn't make ideal caged pets for Mr. B. at school. Ugh. This book, blessedly out of print, should remind us of what bozos we can be when we presume to team up with God and run the planet as a taut ship for the greater glory of our nearly divine intelligence. Ugh—and yet again, ugh.

Birds of My Childhood

I have always loved birds, and am told that, in ages past, I must have been one. But I don't believe in transmigration of souls, nor in the theory that birds were at one time reptiles and have developed themselves into their present higher form of life. I am content to accept the unquestioning creed of my little son, who maintains that, "As the Bible says 'God on the fifth day created every winged fowl after their kind,' it is no use saying that He *didn't!*"

. . . Moses belied his name, for he was by no means "very meek," but combative and resistant. At first there was no taming him. Though not fully fledged, his beak and claws needed no further development. When any one approached, his invariable proceeding was to lean back, standing on one leg, with a wing up-lifted, his curved beak in position for striking, and one sharp-clawed leg held out like a sword ready to grab everything in the shape of a finger that might present itself. I had to adopt the starvation principle, the bread-and-water of affliction, and I met with eminent success.

After a week of meagre rations, it dawned upon

Moses that I was not a foe, but a friend—a friend who represented unlimited food, including dead sparrows, and the fierce glance began to fade from the beautiful eyes when I approached; and one morning he let me treat him to pieces of raw liver with one hand, and stroke his head and glossy back with the other.

I succeeded in rearing Moses, and when the summer-holidays began I took him home, where I kept him on the leads. He used to sit on my arm like a parrot, and never attempted violence or escape. But, alas! one morning I missed him. The cage door had been left slightly open; he had pushed against it, hopped out, and perhaps, hearing the call of some bird that recalled his mother's cry, had used his wings (they were not clipped) and soared away, doubtless surprised to find that he could fly so well without any practice.

Of course, I kept an owlet at school; but he was a failure. He had a trick of lying on his back and hissing like a cat, clawing with both legs if annoyed, which he often was. This habit I could have mitigated in time, had I been able to feed him properly. But this I could not do; for the mice-larder was frequently bare, and young sparrows were not always forthcoming; and as a fair proportion of "fur and feathers" are necessary to an owlet's existence, he pined away on a raw-flesh dietary, and died. *Requiescat in pace.*

Jays are pretty birds, but we found them a decided nuisance. They were not popular. Their gape is prodigious, and they are always craving for food. You cannot look at them when young, without their uttering a peculiar and irritatingly hungry cry; and do what you will you cannot satisfy them. "Oliver Twists" we called them, forgetting that it was only once that poor Oliver asked for "more."

THE SEA AND THE JUNGLE
BY H. M. TOMLINSON

AFOOT IN ENGLAND
BY W. H. HUDSON

Here we have a couple of thunderstorms and a couple of ways of looking at man and nature. Tomlinson, on board a ship during a typhoon, cannot help but describe the storm's passage over the ship as some sort of grand battle, in which the noble-prowed vessel cleaves and routs and shames the huge forces of nature. His boat doesn't just stay afloat through a storm; rather, the sturdy, well-designed devices of man clobber the impudent attack of a stupid and hostile power. It seems pretty forced and ridiculous, this perspective, doesn't it? I mean, sure, congratulations on not sinking and all, but take it easy. . . .

Hudson, on the other hand, enjoys the passage of a storm for what it is. He would be mystified by the idea that thunder and lightning were waging some kind of war against him, a war he could "win" by holding up a hand and striking a defiant pose and surviving the tempest. To Hudson, it's simple: Sometimes it rains; sometimes the sun shines; sometimes it's cloudy. Whatever. He's just a small fellow privileged to stand around and watch, perhaps even to understand a little (water density of rain clouds? temperature in sunlight at this or that season or time of day?), but certainly not to wage any battles, much less win them.

The gale was dumb till it met and was torn in our harsh opposition, shouting and moaning then in anger and torment as we steadily pressed our iron into its ponderable body. You could imagine the flawless flood of air pouring silently express till it met our pillars and pinnacles, and then flying past rift, the thousand punctures instantly spreading into long shrieking lacerations. The wounds and mouths were so many, loud, and poignant, that you wondered you could not see them. Our structure was full of voices, but the weighty body which drove against our shrouds and funnel guys, and kept them strongly vibrating, was curiously invisible. The hard jets of air spurted hissing through the winches. The sound in the shrouds and stays began like that of something tearing, and rose to a high keening. The deeper notes were amidships, in the alleyways and round the engine-room casing; but there the ship itself contributed a note, a metallic murmur so profound that it was felt as a tremor rather than heard. It was almost below human hearing. It was the hollow ship resonant, the steel walls, decks, and bulkheads quivering under the drumming of the seas, and the regular throws of the crank-shaft far below.

—*H. M. Tomlinson*

But, no, there was one more, marvellous as any—the experience of a day of days, one of those rare days when nature appears to us spiritualised and is no longer nature, when that which had transfigured this visible world is in us too, and it becomes possible to believe—it is almost a conviction—that the burning and shining spirit seen and recognised in one among a thousand we have known is in all of us and in all things. In such moments it is possible to go beyond even the most advanced of the modern physicists who holds that force alone exists, that matter is but a disguise, a shadow and delusion; for we may add that force itself—that which we call force or energy—is but a semblance and shadow of the universal soul.

The change in the weather was not sudden; the furious winds dropped gradually; the clouds floated higher in the heavens, and were of a lighter grey; there were wider breaks in them, showing the lucid blue beyond; and the sea grew quieter. It had raved and roared too long, beating against the iron walls that held it back, and was now spent and fallen into an uneasy sleep, but still moved uneasily and moaned a little. Then all at once summer returned, coming like a thief in the night, for when it was morning the sun rose in splendour and power in a sky without a cloud on its vast azure expanse, on a calm sea with no motion but that scarcely perceptible rise and fall as of one that sleeps. As the sun rose higher the air grew warmer until it was full summer heat, but although a "visible heat," it was never oppressive; for all that day we were abroad, and as the tide ebbed a new country that was neither earth nor sea was disclosed, an infinite expanse of pale yellow sand stretching away on either side, and further and further out until it mingled and melted into the sparkling water and faintly seen line of foam on the horizon. And over all—the distant sea, the ridge of low dunes marking where the earth ended, and the flat yellow expanse between—there brooded a soft bluish silvery haze. A haze that blotted nothing out, but blended and interfused them all until earth and air and sea and sands were scarcely distinguishable. The effect, delicate, mysterious, unearthly, cannot be described.

> Ethereal gauze . . .
> Visible heat, air-water, and dry sea,
> Last conquest of the eye . . .
> Sun-dust,
> Aerial surf upon the shores of earth,
> Ethereal estuary, frith of light. . . .
> Bird of the sun, transparent-winged.

Do we not see that words fail as pigments do—that the effect is too coarse, since in describing it we put it before the mental eye as something distinctly visible, a thing of itself and separate. But it is not so in nature; the effect is of something almost invisible and is yet a part of all and makes all things—sky and sea and land—as unsubstantial as itself. Even living, moving things had that aspect. Far out on the lowest furthest strip of sand, which appeared to be on a level with the sea, gulls were seen standing in twos and threes and small groups and in rows; but they did not look like gulls—familiar birds, gull-shaped with grey and white plumage. They appeared twice as big as gulls, and were of a dazzling whiteness and of no definite shape: though standing still they had motion, an effect of the quivering dancing air, the "visible heat"; at rest, they were seen now as separate objects; then as one with the silver sparkle on the sea; and when they rose and floated away they were no longer shining and white, but like pale shadows of winged forms faintly visible in the haze.

They were not birds but spirits—beings that lived in or were passing through the world and now, like the heat, made visible; and I, standing far out on the sparkling sands, with the sparkling sea on one side and the line of dunes, indistinctly seen as land, on the other, was one of them; and if any person had looked at me from a distance he would have seen me as a formless shining white being standing by the sea, and then perhaps as a winged shadow floating in the haze. It was only necessary to put out one's arms to float. That was the effect on my mind: this natural world was changed to a supernatural, and there was no more matter nor force in sea or land nor in the heavens above, but only spirit.

—W. H. Hudson

Hyena

BY JOANNA GREENFIELD

Often, good writers use language as a way of reducing distance, of pulling us closer to experiences that may have occurred twenty or seventy-five or three thousand years ago in other places. They make it seem as if things were happening right now, right here, to us.

"To us" is perhaps the key to reading this next piece, because here the writer seems to be using language—almost desperately—to establish distance. Weirder still, she is establishing distance between us (and herself with us) and an experience that happened to her. No guessing about what Edgar Allan Poe's life was like and then rendering it in words that duplicate those guesses for us. No—this woman watched a hyena as it was eating her, and now she is writing about it, and the result of reading what she wrote is feeling not only that we didn't experience it, but also that in a way she herself did not.

I'm not saying we think she's lying or anything—we

believe readily enough that she's got the scars and limps she says she has; we believe the facts. But the experience— the nitty-gritty horror of it—is pushed away from us, and from herself, by the cool, almost disbelieving way she writes about what she says she was coolly thinking as she watched the animal chew its way up her bloody-to-the-bone arm. No way was she that conscious, we say. That's just writing, and writing done after that fact, looking back.

But do we have the right to say this? Shouldn't we consider, for a moment, that maybe the usual writer's usual reproduction of "experience"—which in this case would be full of action and gore and horror—could be a convention of writing, a habit of reading? Isn't it possible that when something really nasty and dangerous happens to us, we retreat from our bodies into our mind and, as if to say, "No, this can't be real!" begin to reflect upon it, like a— well, like a writer or something? Maybe. Maybe this is what happened here, with this hyena eating its way up this woman's arm. Then again, maybe the experience was just too horrible for her to tell us the truth-of-the-moment about. We'll just have to read and decide. Either way, it's pretty incredible stuff.

not hormonally sedated, she lunged at passersby, swatting her claws through the chicken wire.

"You're so beautiful."

She purred, and rubbed against the mesh. The men said you could stroke her like a house cat when she was in these moods. I wanted to touch her, a leopard from the oases of Israel's last deserts, but I stayed away, in case she changed her mind, and squatted out of reach to talk to her. I didn't want to force her to defend herself.

It might have been the attention I gave the leopard, but Efa was in a frenzy of *"Mmmaaaaaaaa"s* when I returned to his cage. He crouched like a baby, begging for something. I filled a water tray and unlatched the door that opened into a corridor running between the cage and the corral, then I closed it. If only I'd just squirted the hose into the cage, but instead I unlatched the cage door and bent over to put the dish down, talking to him. The mind, I found, is strange. It shut off during the attack, while my body continued to act, without thought or even sight. I don't remember him sinking his teeth into my arm, though I heard a little grating noise as his teeth chewed into the bone.

Everything was black and slow and exploding in

my stomach. Vision returned gradually, like an ancient black-and-white television pulling dots and flashes to the center for a picture. I saw at a remove the hyena inside my right arm, and my other arm banging him on the head. My body, in the absence of a mind, had decided that this was the best thing to do. And scream. Scream in a thin angry hysteria that didn't sound like me. Where was everyone? My mind was so calm and remote that I frightened myself, but my stomach twisted. I hit harder, remembering the others he'd nipped. He'd always let go.

Efa blinked and surged back, jerking me forward. I stumbled out of my sandals into the sand, thinking, with fresh anxiety, I'll burn my feet. I tried to kick him between the legs, but it was awkward, and he was pulling me down by the arm, down and back into the cage. When I came back from Africa the first time, I took a class in self-defense so I'd feel safer with all the soldiers, guerrilla warriors, and policemen when I returned. I remembered the move I'd vowed to use on any attacker: a stab and grab at the jugular, to snap it inside the skin. But the hyena has callused skin on its throat, thick and rough, like eczema. I lost hope and felt the slowness of this death to be the worst insult. Hyenas don't kill fast, and I could end up in the sand watching my entrails get pulled through a cut in my stomach and eaten like spaghetti, with tugs and jerks. I started to get mad, an unfamiliar feeling creeping in to add an acid burn to the chill of my stomach. Another removal from myself. I never let myself get mad. I want peace. I tried to pinch his nostrils so he'd let go of my arm to breathe, but he shook his head, pulling me deeper into the cage.

I think it was then that he took out the first piece from my arm and swallowed it without breathing, because a terror of movement settled in me at that moment and lasted for months. He moved up the arm, and all the time those black, blank eyes evaluated me, like a shark's, calm and almost friendly. By this time, my right arm was a mangled mess of flesh, pushed-out globs of fat, and flashes of bone two inches long, but my slow TV mind, watching, saw it as whole, just trapped in the hyena's mouth, in a tug-of-war like the one I used to play with my dogs—only it was my arm now instead of a sock. It didn't hurt. It never did.

The hyena looked up at me with those indescribable eyes and surged back again, nearly pulling me onto his face. I remembered self-defense class and the first lesson: "Poke the cockroach in the eyes." All the

women had squealed, except me. "Ooooh, I could
never do that." Ha, I'd thought. Anyone who wants to
kill me has no right to live. I'd poke him in the eyes.

I looked at those eyes with my fingers poised to jab. It
was for my family and my friends that I stuck my fingers in his eyes. I just wanted to stop watching myself
get eaten, either be dead and at peace or be gone, but
other lives were connected to mine. I'm not sure if I
did more than touch them gently before he let go and
whipped past me to cower against the door to the outside, the Negev desert.

Events like this teach you yourself. We all think we
know what we would do, hero or coward, strong or
weak. I expected strength, and the memory of my tin-
whistle scream curdles my blood, but I am proud of
the stupid thing I did next. He cowered and whim-
pered and essentially apologized, still with those blank
unmoving eyes, and I stood still for a second. My arm
felt light and shrunken, as if half of it were gone, but
I didn't look. From the corridor, I had a choice of two
doors: the one through which I'd entered, leading
back to the desert, and the one opening onto the corral. I didn't think I could bend over him and unlatch
the door to the desert. He'd just reach up and clamp

onto my stomach. And I didn't want to open the door to the corral, or he'd drag me in and be able to attack the men if they ever came to help me. My body, still in control, made the good hand grab the bad elbow, and I beat him with my own arm, as if I had ripped it free to use as a club. "No!" I shouted. "No, no!" *Lo lo lo*, in Hebrew. I might even have said "Bad boy," but I hope not. It was the beating that damaged my hand permanently. I must have hit him hard enough to crush a ligament, because there is a lump on my hand to this day, five years later, but he didn't even blink. He came around behind me and grabbed my right leg, and again there was no pain—just the feeling that he and I were playing tug-of-war with my body—but I was afraid to pull too hard on the leg. He pulled the leg up, stretching me out in a line from the door, where I clung with the good hand to the mesh, like a dancer at the barre. It felt almost good, as if the whole thing were nearer to being over. In three moves I didn't feel, he took out most of the calf.

I opened the door to the desert and he ran out, with a quick shove that staggered me. I couldn't move the right leg, just crutched myself along on it into the Negev. He waited for me. The cold in my stomach was stabbing my breath away. The hyena and I were bonded now. Even if someone did come to help, there was still something left to finish between us. I was marked—his. I saw, in color, that he was going to knock me over, and I thought, in black-and-white, No, don't, you'll hurt my leg, I should keep it still.

A workman stood by a shed uphill, leaning on a tool in the sand. He watched me walk toward the office, with the hyena ahead and looking back at me. He was the only spectator I noticed, though I was told later, in the hospital, that some tourists, there to see the animals, were screaming for help, and three— or was it five?—soldiers had had their machine guns aimed at us throughout the whole thing. Israeli soldiers carry their arms everywhere when they're in uniform; but they must have been afraid to shoot. I don't know. Stories get told afterward. I didn't see anyone except the workman, looking on impassively, and the leopard, pacing inside her fence, roaring a little, with the peace of her heat gone as suddenly as it had appeared.

THE SNAKE

BY JOHN CROMPTON

John Crompton, a British gentleman of the old school who spent most of the first half of this century traveling from one civic post to another in places that reeked of Empire (India, China, South Africa), always seems to know a chap who had a rather peculiar experience with just the sort of creature that happens to be under discussion. . . . Some unregistered amount of time later, he finishes his intriguing tale, pauses politely to allow you to digest it (not the best choice of words, as so many of Crompton's stories have to do with how animals kill and consume one another), and then, after rattling off a few alarming facts with a very droll sureness, he mentions yet another chap who once had the misfortune of testing that very theory, although quite by accident, when he found himself across a clearing from a king cobra one moonlit night about two hundred miles north of Calcutta. . . .

Anecdotes, anecdotes, anecdotes. John Crompton, author of six books on specific types of animals, was not a scientist, and probably wouldn't have even called himself a naturalist. But he was a listener, and when he heard a good story, he knew it. If the story happened to have something to do with a certain interesting insect or reptile, Crompton made it his business to learn a bit about the creature and by all means to keep track of every story he heard thereafter that remotely touched on the subject. Eventually, finding himself with a little time on his hands, he decided to jot down a book-sort-of-thing, and then another, and another . . . and before long we had six of the strangest, most casually knowledgeable, irreverently witty nature books ever written. Oh, sure, now and then a humorless scientist-type would quibble with this or that assertion or anecdote, but, frankly, anyone who has read John Crompton on one subject will gladly read him on another over almost any other author, no matter how scientifically qualified. The ear is drawn to good, precise sentences and paragraphs with a tone and content all their own. Read here just some of what Crompton had to say on the topic of poison in snakes, and see if you can resist finding his snake book and reading the rest of it. After that, there seems to be one about wasps or something, and one about ants—and pretty soon, you'll be in the ter-

rible state of having devoured (another unfortunate word, perhaps) all there is of John Crompton's brand of decidedly unstuffy nature writing. You'll probably wait a while and start again.

How it came about that snakes manufactured poison is a mystery. Over periods their saliva, a mild digestive juice like our own, was converted into a poison that defies analysis even today. It was not forced upon them by the survival competition; they could have caught and lived on prey without using poison just as the thousands of non-poisonous snakes still do. Poison to a snake is merely a luxury; it enables it to get its food with very little effort, no more effort than one bite. And why only snakes? Cats, for instance, would be greatly helped; no running fights with large, fierce rats or tussles with grown rabbits—just a bite and no more effort needed. In fact, it would be an assistance to all the carnivorae—though it would be a two-edged weapon when they fought each other. But, of the vertebrates, unpredictable Nature selected only snakes (and one lizard). One wonders also why Nature, with some snakes, concocted poison of such extreme potency.

In the conversion of saliva into poison one might suppose that a fixed process took place. It did not; some snakes manufactured a poison different in every respect from that of the others, as different as arsenic is from strychnine, and having different effects. One poison acts on the nerves, the other on the blood.

The makers of the nerve poison include the mambas and the cobras and their venom is called neurotoxic. Vipers (adders) and rattlesnakes manufacture the blood poison, which is known as haemolytic. Both poisons are unpleasant, but by far the more unpleasant is the blood poison. It is said that the nerve poison is the more primitive of the two, that the blood poison is, so to speak, a newer product from an improved formula. Be that as it may, the nerve poison does its business with man far more quickly than the blood poison. This, however, means nothing. Snakes did not acquire their poison for use against man but for use against prey such as rats and mice, and the effect on these of viperine poison is almost immediate.

As a slight complication it so happens that the two poisons are rarely quite pure. So the nerve poison of the cobras, etc. usually possesses a trace of the blood poison of the vipers, and vice versa. But it is legitimate, as well as convenient, to class the two poisons as two different concoctions.

. . . When striking, a snake likes to hang on like a bulldog whilst its fangs pump the full dose of poison into the flesh. This rarely happens with a man, for he is usually able to beat the reptile off. Even so, he must be quick. A cobra, for instance, can squirt out twelve drops of poison in a few seconds, and one drop can be fatal to an adult human being.

The injection of suitable antivenine (and there is not antivenine for *every* type of snake poison), if given in time, will neutralize any snake poison, but if (this is very rare) a fang should inject poison direct into a vein, death may occur in one minute. This, in fact, has happened.

On being bitten by a snake possessing neurotoxic poison, such as a cobra, the usual symptoms are a searing pain from the wound itself, then a weakness in the legs, gradually developing into incapability of making any movement at all. Saliva dribbles from the mouth owing to the paralysis of the muscles of the mouth. The tongue, too, becomes paralysed and the victim, though able to hear, is unable to speak. He begins to vomit, and has difficulty in breathing. This difficulty increases until he is suffocating, and finally breathing stops altogether. Meanwhile the heart has been racing on, and it continues to beat for a considerable time after breathing has stopped.

. . . It is not easy to obtain data of the symptoms of poisoning by the deadlier snakes. Snakes can be made to bite unfortunate experimental animals, but these animals, whether they live or die, cannot tell us their symptoms, and post-mortems get us little further. Not a few men have been bitten by the bad types of snakes and recovered, and here, one would think, would be an ideal source of knowledge. Not a bit; the majority remember next to nothing. Besides other sufferings, the subject is in a state of terror, and terrified men are not in a state of mind to note and memorize symptoms.

And one can hardly experiment on human beings. Volunteers for, say, mamba poisoning would be hard to come by. Nevertheless one brave soul *did* undergo such a test. Some time ago, a Dr. Eizenberger decided to experiment on himself. He did not propose, however, to kill himself, and used such a small dose that he thought the effect would be negligible—he could always use a larger dose if this one proved to have no effect. He took one drop of the venom of the green

mamba of West Africa *(Dendraspis viridis).* This drop
he diluted with ten times the quantity of water, and of
this very weak solution he only injected 0.2 cc. into
his forearm.

A burning sensation was felt immediately, and five
minutes later there was a swelling over the puncture,
accompanied by itching. Soon he knew that his nerves
were affected. Ordinary everyday noises became deaf-
ening. His car seemed to make such a din, bumping
and banging, and he thought a tire must be punctured
and got out to look. Saliva flowed copiously in his
mouth and he felt as if he were intoxicated. Soon
(about fifteen minutes after the injection) he was seized
with nausea and weakness and decided the time had
come to put an end to this experiment and do what he
could to stop any further absorption of the venom. It
was far too late, but he applied a tourniquet, cut open
the swelling and soused the bleeding cut with a hot
solution of permanganate.

His chin, lips and the tip of his tongue became
numb. This numbness spread over his face and down
his throat. His eyes and the base of his tongue became
painful, and he lost all feeling in his fingers and toes.
His ears started to drum and the pain and stiffness of
his tongue travelled down his throat, which became

acutely sore. It became difficult to talk or swallow, and difficult and painful to breathe.

Alarmed and fearing collapse, Doctor Eizenberger gave himself an injection of strychnine, which had a good effect and improved his circulation.

Then his hand and forearm swelled up and the parts that had been numb became painful. After five hours a touch on any part of his body was painful, and swallowing was very difficult. But the worst was over. He went to bed and passed the night in a feverish state. In the morning his tongue and throat still pained, but these discomforts gradually passed off.

He made a complete recovery, and this is the case with all who are bitten by neurotoxic snakes and escape death.

THE GLOW-WORM
AND OTHER BEETLES

BY JEAN-HENRI FABRE

Not only is Fabre probably the greatest nature writer ever to publish a paragraph, he may also have been the greatest natural scientist. Nowhere else do vast general joy and minute precision of thought and action coexist so perfectly. Fabre loves his insects, adores them all the more—with the right mix of amazement and exact belief—for all the intricate little facts he discovers, tests, and puts together for himself and us. He kills and maims individual insects and intrudes on whole populations, but always it is clear that he does so delicately, kindly—respectfully. His respect is boundless, for the Creator, for the design of the processes of nature and of the bodies of the insects themselves, and even for the spirit of inquiry with which he was blessed. And respect, if not outright love, is what he wants to leave us with, too. He does. We cannot help but share his wonder, his delight, his analytical questioning, his joy in solutions, his ultimate pleasure that it all works the way it does. So he writes it all down, then he withdraws. We read and, like him, withdraw. But always, like him, we will keep watching, with amazement and new knowledge, forever.

...We French have the expression "Naked as a worm," to point to the lack of any defensive covering. Now the Lampyris is clothed, that is to say, he wears an epidermis of some consistency; moreover, he is rather richly coloured: his body is dark brown all over, set off with pale pink on the thorax, especially on the lower surface. Finally, each segment is decked at the hinder edge with two spots of a fairly bright red. A costume like this was never worn by a worm.

Let us leave this ill-chosen denomination and ask ourselves what the Lampyris feeds upon. That master of the art of gastronomy, Brillat-Savarin, said:

"Show me what you eat and I will tell you what you are."

A similar question should be addressed, by way of a preliminary, to every insect whose habits we propose to study, for, from the least to the greatest in the zoological progression, the stomach sways the world; the data supplied by food are the chief of all the documents of life. Well, in spite of his innocent appearance, the Lampyris is an eater of flesh, a hunter of game; and he follows his calling with rare villainy. His regular prey is the Snail.

This detail has long been known to entomologists. What is not so well-known, what is not known at all yet, to judge by what I have read, is the curious method of attack, of which I have seen no other instance anywhere.

Before he begins to feast, the Glow-worm administers an anæsthetic: he chloroforms his victim, rivalling in the process the wonders of our modern surgery, which renders the patient insensible before operating on him. The usual game is a small Snail hardly the size of a cherry, such as, for instance, *Helix variabilis*, DRAP., who, in the hot weather, collects in clusters on the stiff stubble and on other long, dry stalks, by the roadside, and there remains motionless, in profound meditation, throughout the scorching summer days. It is in some such resting-place as this that I have often been privileged to light upon the Lampyris banqueting on the prey which he had just paralyzed on its shaky support by his surgical artifices.

But he is familiar with other preserves. He frequents the edges of the irrigating-ditches, with their cool soil, their varied vegetation, a favourite haunt of the mollusc. Here, he treats the game on the ground; and, under these conditions, it is easy for me to rear him at home and to follow the operator's performance down to the smallest detail.

I will try to make the reader a witness of the strange sight. I place a little grass in a wide glass jar. In this I install a few Glow-worms and a provision of Snails of a suitable size, neither too large nor too small, chiefly *Helix variabilis*. We must be patient and wait. Above all, we must keep an assiduous watch, for the desired events come unexpectedly and do not last long.

Here we are at last. The Glow-worm for a moment investigates the prey, which, according to its habit, is wholly withdrawn in the shell, except the edge of the mantle, which projects slightly. Then the hunter's weapon is drawn, a very simple weapon, but one that cannot be plainly perceived without the aid of a lens. It consists of two mandibles bent back powerfully into a hook, very sharp and as thin as a hair. The microscope reveals the presence of a slender groove running throughout the length. And that is all.

The insect repeatedly taps the Snail's mantle with its instrument. It all happens with such gentleness as to suggest kisses rather than bites. As children, teasing one another, we used to talk of "tweaksies" to express a slight squeeze of the finger-tips, something more like a tickling than a serious pinch. Let us use that word. In conversing with animals, language loses nothing by remaining juvenile. It is the right way for the simple to understand one another.

The Lampyris doles out his tweaks. He distributes them methodically, without hurrying, and takes a brief rest after each of them, as though he wished to ascertain the effect produced. Their number is not great: half-a-dozen, at most, to subdue the prey and deprive it of all power of movement. That other pinches are administered later, at the time of eating, seems very likely, but I cannot say anything for certain, because the sequel escapes me. The first few, however—there are never many—are enough to impart inertia and loss of all feeling to the mollusc, thanks to the prompt, I might almost say, lightning methods of the Lampyris, who, beyond a doubt, instils some poison or other by means of his grooved hooks.

Here is the proof of the sudden efficacity of those twitches, so mild in appearance: I take the Snail from the Lampyris, who has operated on the edge of the mantle some four or five times. I prick him with a fine needle in the fore-part, which the animal, shrunk into its shell, still leaves exposed. There is no quiver of the wounded tissues, no reaction against the brutality of the needle. A corpse itself could not give fewer signs of life.

Here is something even more conclusive: chance occasionally gives me Snails attacked by the Lampyris while they are creeping along, the foot slowly crawling, the tentacles swollen to their full extent. A few disordered movements betray a brief excitement on the part of the mollusc and then everything ceases: the foot no longer slugs; the front-part loses its graceful swan-neck curve; the tentacles become limp and give way under their weight, dangling feebly like a broken stick. This conditions persists.

Is the Snail really dead? Not at all, for I am free to resuscitate the seeming corpse. After two or three days of that singular condition which is no longer life and yet not death, I isolate the patient and, although this is not really necessary to success, I give him a douche which will represent the shower so dear to the able-bodied mollusc. In about a couple of days, my prisoner, but lately injured by the Glow-worm's treachery, is restored to his normal state. He revives, in a manner; he recovers movement and sensibility. He is affected by the stimulus of a needle; he shifts his place, crawls, puts out his tentacles, as though nothing unusual had occurred. The general torpor, a sort of deep drunkenness, has vanished outright. The dead returns to life. What name shall we give to that form of existence which, for a time, abolishes the power of movement and the sense of pain? I can see but one that is approximately suitable: anæsthesia. The exploits of a host of Wasps whose flesh-eating grubs are provided with meat that is motionless though not dead have taught us the skilful art of the paralyzing insect, which numbs the locomotory nerve-centres with its venom. We have now a humble little animal that first produces complete anæsthesia in its patient. Human science did not in reality invent this art, which is one of the wonders of our latter-day surgery. Much earlier, far back in the centuries, the Lampyris and, apparently, others knew it as well. The animal's knowledge had a long start [over] ours; the method alone has changed. Our operators proceed by making us inhale the fumes of ether or chloroform; the insect proceeds by injecting a special virus that comes from the mandibular fangs in infinitesimal doses. Might we not one day be able to benefit by this hint? What glorious discoveries the future would have in store for us, if we understood the beastie's secrets better!

ABYSS: THE DEEP SEA AND THE CREATURES THAT LIVE IN IT

BY C. P. IDYLL

C. P. Idyll's long book explores everything from the geology of mountain ranges seven miles beneath the water to the odd biochemistry of organic luminescence in fish that live four miles down under water pressure that would turn a sixteen-wheel semi into a twist of flattened junk metal in less than a second. It is a rich book full of sections that are sometimes dull in their analytical detail, and sometimes incredibly fascinating in their exposure of secret lives most of us have never even wondered about. It is the brief tale of one of the latter that is included here, mostly, I confess, because it is so gross it's unbelievably cool. We all need a good gross detail now and then. Otherwise, we might get a little too poetic about all of these pretty trees and sparkling rivers and stuff.

In shallow water, fish eat sea urchins if they can get past their spines. Even *Diadema*, with its formidable black armor, is the victim of some marine animals. The helmet shell, *Cassis*, a big snail of tropic seas, eats them, as do some of the stronger and braver fishes. Sea urchins are the primary food of sea otters off the coast of California. Other urchins are eaten by starfish, which surround smaller individuals with their everted stomachs; if the sea urchin is too big to permit this, the starfish forces its stomach down the mouth of the unfortunate victim, digesting it from the inside.

In the United States, where abundance has made people finicky about their food, the idea of cracking open a sea urchin and spooning out the raw eggs is looked on with horror. In other parts of the world they are a delicacy. In Mediterranean countries sea urchins are peddled in the streets. Vendors in Marseilles, Naples, and other ports supply vinegar with the urchins for the buyer to sprinkle over the eggs, which he sucks raw from the shell. In Barbados, urchins are called sea eggs and their roe is sold in the streets in little cones fashioned from leaves. Hotels serve them for breakfast cooked like scrambled eggs.

The name "echinoderm" is not very appropriate for the sea cucumbers, which have surfaces as far removed from spininess as could be conceived. They are usually markedly soft and yielding, with a slimy feel, and several of their habits are as repugnant as their appearance. First of all, one of the sea cucumber's methods of self-protection is to eject a good part of its viscera when disturbed. This presumably confuses and repels the would-be predator, and the sea urchin placidly grows a new set of interior plumbing. Another defense mechanism is the discharge of sticky white threads from the anus; these swell in the water and prevent a predator from seizing the sea cucumber. This trick gives the name of cotton spinner to the animal. The sea cucumber carries its respiratory gills inside the anus too, and, to cap the story, several small animals, including the little fish *Carapus*, commonly make their home inside this strange gill chamber.

. . . These amazing color changes in the octopus, and in all cephalopods, are produced by tiny spots of pigment in the skin. The pigment cells, called chromatophores, are very small and transparent and are filled with a fluid in which are suspended granules of pigment. Attached to the very elastic walls of the chromatophores are radially arranged muscle fibers. When these fibers are at rest, the pigment cells are contracted to a very small size, almost disappearing in the skin of the animal. The muscles can pull out the chromatophores to a much greater size, spreading the color over a wide area of the skin. In combination, many of the pigment cells lend their color to a large or a small area of the skin. Douglas Wilson says: "It is a fine sight to watch a shoal of these elongated creatures and see their skins shimmering as the tiny spots of color rapidly expand and contract."

The cuttlefish *Sepia* is probably the most skillful of the whole clever group at producing color changes. *Sepia* has chromatophores of three colors arranged in three layers beneath its transparent skin. The top layer contains bright yellow cells, the next layer orange-red cells, and the third layer dark brown, nearly black, cells. Beneath these layers of contractile cells is a basal layer of brilliant iridocytes whose beautiful iridescence forms the background for the other colors. *Sepia* can make itself white by contracting all the cells, or yellow by contracting all but the top layer of cells, or it can darken its skin by exhibiting only the third layer. It can also expand some of each kind of chromatophore, completely or partially, in infinite variation and thus produce a rainbow kaleidoscope of color to suit all occasions. Guided by the eye, the central nervous system controls the slim muscle fibers that work the

chromatophores, and the color of the animal is therefore under its full control. The speed with which color
changes can be made greatly exceeds anything elsewhere in the animal kingdom, and a color cell can
change from a condition of full contraction to
full expansion—as much as sixty times its original
diameter—in two thirds of a second. The muscle
fibers seem to be immune to fatigue. Scientists found
that the muscles seemed to work as efficiently as ever
after being stimulated for 30 minutes with electric
shocks at the rate of thirty per second.

At rest the cuttlefish sends continuous waves of
color over its skin, the shifting of shades and the generally striped pattern undoubtedly making it more difficult for a predator to keep the little animal in focus.
While swimming, the cuttlefish can alter its color to
suit the background. In *Kingdom of the Octopus*, Frank
Lane reports observations by Joyce Allan, an Australian biologist, who "watched some small Australian
cuttlefish swimming slowly about an aquarium containing variously colored objects. As the cuttles passed
over dark, reddish brown rock, they matched its color
perfectly. A few inches away there was some dead
coral, and as the cuttles passed over it they turned a
light grey. Then, in turn, light brown for sand, green-

brown for weeds, and back again to the reddish-brown of the rock."

Dr. William Holmes, a British biologist, published results of interesting experiments on the color changes of *Sepia officinalis*. In a large aquarium tank at the Plymouth Laboratory the back of the squid was dark brown, nearly a solid color down the middle but with irregular stripes down the sides that broke up the outline of the animal against its background. When it lay on the sand the animal assumed a light mottled appearance like the sand itself; in addition, it threw up sand with its fins so that particles fell on the edges of its body, obliterating its outline. In a black tank the squid assumed a very dark color. If now a white piece of porcelain was put in the tank near it, the animal produced an astonishing square patch of white on its back against the dark skin to mimic the porcelain. In a well-lighted aquarium having a strongly contrasted background of light and dark stones on the bottom, a broad, very white stripe appeared laterally across the back of the animal. When disturbed, the squid produced two black spots on its back, always in the same position. If the annoyance persisted, the animal accentuated the black spots by lightening the rest of its skin so that the spots stood out vividly against the iridescent white body. Often at this point the squid would contract its body suddenly and shoot away with an abrupt squirt of its siphon, at the same time flashing a dark color over its body. This performance left the observer staring at the place where the white animal with the black spots had been an instant before, while the squid was safely elsewhere.

Desert Solitaire

BY EDWARD ABBEY

Edward Abbey's opening for this book explains perfectly the finest feature of our most natural slack-jawed, open-minded response to nature: love, and the need for love's simple directness. Or, if that's too gooey for you, acceptance, or awed approval, or something else that says how ready we are to like what we find. Few people led blindfolded to the lip of a canyon or sea bluff are so cranky that they stand there determined to dislike what they are about to have revealed to them. No, generally we are optimists about nature. Maybe we're scared to go to parties because we always seem to dislike almost everyone we meet; maybe we are proud skeptics about enthusiasms our friends adopt and prattle to us about—but we usually can't help but be all ready to find a macaw beautiful or a tall forest peaceful.

Edward Abbey himself was not exactly a peaceful tree-hugger, not your normal, polite "nature lover" (the adjective

*"hoodoo" in this piece is kind of a tip-off). He was a lead-
ing advocate of what was called deep ecology and ecodefense, by which he and others meant that it was okay to
battle the destruction of the environment by destroying the
tools of destruction first. Ecodefense warriors (also called
ecoterrorists) dynamited bulldozers, drove backhoes off
cliffs into deep lakes, sabotaged cranes and cement mix-
ers, and notified timber companies that the trees the company lumberjacks were about to cut down and ship to
sawmills had been randomly spiked with huge, unde-
tectable nails that would shatter the sawmill's blades and
shut down production for days. Abbey's message: Leave
Nature Alone! Enjoy it, but let it be what it is. (And
while you're at it, be what you are too—cook that bacon
guilt-free, humankind!) We can't make nature any better,
and destroying it to make our lives superficially more
comfy is a crime far worse than blowing up some timber
company's fleet of graders and dozers.*

THE FIRST MORNING

This is the most beautiful place on earth.

There are many such places. Every man, every
woman, carries in heart and mind the image of the

ideal place, the right place, the one true home, known or unknown, actual or visionary. A houseboat in Kashmir, a view down Atlantic Avenue in Brooklyn, a gray gothic farmhouse two stories high at the end of a red dog road in the Allegheny Mountains, a cabin on the shore of a blue lake in spruce and fir country, a greasy alley near the Hoboken waterfront, or even, possibly, for those of a less demanding sensibility, the world to be seen from a comfortable apartment high in the tender, velvety smog of Manhattan, Chicago, Paris, Tokyo, Rio or Rome—there's no limit to the human capacity for the homing sentiment. Theologians, sky pilots, astronauts have even felt the appeal of home calling to them from up above, in the cold black outback of intersteller space.

For myself I'll take Moab, Utah. I don't mean the town itself, of course, but the country which surrounds it—the canyonlands. The slickrock desert. The red dust and the burnt cliffs and the lonely sky—all that which lies beyond the end of the roads.

The choice became apparent to me this morning when I stepped out of a Park Service housetrailer—my caravan—to watch for the first time in my life the sun come up over the hoodoo stone of Arches National Monument.

I wasn't able to see much of it last night. After driving all day from Albuquerque—450 miles—I reached Moab after dark in cold, windy, clouded weather. At park headquarters north of town I met the superintendent and the chief ranger, the only permanent employees, except for one maintenance man, in this particular unit of America's national park system. After coffee they gave me a key to the housetrailer and directions on how to reach it; I am required to live and work not at headquarters but at this one-man station some twenty miles back in the interior, on my own. The way I wanted it, naturally, or I'd never have asked for the job.

Leaving the headquarters area and the lights of Moab, I drove twelve miles farther north on the highway until I came to a dirt road on the right, where a small wooden sign pointed the way: Arches National Monument Eight Miles. I left the pavement, turned east into the howling wilderness. Wind roaring out of the northwest, black clouds across the stars—all I could see were clumps of brush and scattered junipers along the roadside. Then another modest signboard:

WARNING: QUICKSAND

DO NOT CROSS WASH

WHEN WATER IS RUNNING

The wash looked perfectly dry in my headlights. I drove down, across, up the other side and on into the night. Glimpses of weird humps of pale rock on either side, like petrified elephants, dinosaurs, stone-age hobgoblins. Now and then something alive scurried across the road: kangaroo mice, a jackrabbit, an animal that looked like a cross between a raccoon and a squirrel—the ringtail cat. Farther on a pair of mule deer started from the brush and bounded obliquely through the beams of my lights, raising puffs of dust which the wind, moving faster than my pickup truck, caught and carried ahead of me out of sight into the dark. The road, narrow and rocky, twisted sharply left and right, dipped in and out of tight ravines, climbing by degrees toward a summit which I would see only in the light of the coming day.

Snow was swirling through the air when I crossed the unfenced line and passed the boundary marker of the park. A quarter-mile beyond I found the ranger station—a wide place in the road, an informational display under a lean-to shelter, and fifty yards away the little tin government housetrailer where I would be living for the next six months.

A cold night, a cold wind, the snow falling like confetti. In the lights of the truck I unlocked the housetrailer, got out bedroll and baggage and moved in. By flashlight I found the bed, unrolled my sleeping bag, pulled off my boots and crawled in and went to sleep at once. The last I knew was the shaking of the trailer in the wind and the sound, from inside, of hungry mice scampering around with the good news that their long lean lonesome winter was over—their friend and provider had finally arrived.

This morning I awake before sunrise, stick my head out of the sack, peer through a frosty window at a scene dim and vague with flowing mists, dark fantastic shapes looming beyond. An unlikely landscape.

I get up, moving about in long underwear and socks, stooping carefully under the low ceiling and the lower doorways of the housetrailer, a machine for living built so efficiently and compactly there's hardly room for a man to breathe. An iron lung it is, with windows and venetian blinds.

The mice are silent, watching me from their hiding places, but the wind is still blowing and outside the ground is covered with snow. Cold as a tomb, a jail, a cave; I lie down on the dusty floor, on the cold linoleum sprinkled with mouse turds, and light the pilot on the butane heater. Once this thing gets going the place warms up fast, in a dense unhealthy way, with a layer of heat under the ceiling where my head is and nothing but frigid air from the knees down. But we've got all the indispensable conveniences: gas cookstove, gas refrigerator, hot water heater, sink with running water (if the pipes aren't frozen), storage cabinets and shelves, everything within arm's reach of everything else. The gas comes from two steel bottles in a shed outside; the water comes by gravity flow from a tank buried in a hill close by. Quite luxurious for the wilds. There's even a shower stall and a flush toilet with a dead rat in the bowl. Pretty soft. My poor mother raised five children without any of these luxuries and might be doing without them yet if it hadn't been for Hitler, war and general prosperity.

Time to get dressed, get out and have a look at the lay of the land, fix a breakfast. I try to pull on my boots but they're stiff as iron from the cold. I light a burner on the stove and hold the boots upside down above the flame until they are malleable enough to force my feet into. I put on a coat and step outside. In the center of the world, God's navel, Abbey's country, the red wasteland.

The sun is not yet in sight but signs of the advent are plain to see. Lavender clouds sail like a fleet of ships across the pale green dawn; each cloud, planed flat on the wind, has a base of fiery gold. Southeast, twenty miles by line of sight, stand the peaks of the

Sierra La Sal, twelve to thirteen thousand feet above sea level, all covered with snow and rosy in the morning sunlight. The air is dry and clear as well as cold; the last fogbanks left over from last night's storm are scudding away like ghosts, fading into nothing before the wind and the sunrise.

The view is open and perfect in all directions except to the west where the ground rises and the skyline is only a few hundred yards away. Looking toward the mountains I can see the dark gorge of the Colorado River five or six miles away, carved through the sandstone mesa, though nothing of the river itself down inside the gorge. Southward, on the far side of the river, lies the Moab valley between thousand-foot walls of rock, with the town of Moab somewhere on the valley floor, too small to be seen from here. Beyond the Moab valley is more canyon and tableland, stretching away to the Blue Mountains fifty miles south. On the north and northwest I see the Roan Cliffs and the Book Cliffs, the two-level face of the Uinta Plateau. Along the foot of those cliffs, maybe thirty miles off, invisible from where I stand, runs U.S. 6–50, a major east-west artery of commerce, traffic and rubbish, and the main line of the Denver–Rio Grande Railroad. To the east, under the spreading sunrise, are more mesas, more canyons, league on league of red cliff and arid tablelands, extending through purple haze over the bulging curve of the planet to the ranges of Colorado—a sea of desert.

Within this vast perimeter, in the middle ground and foreground of the picture, a rather personal demesne, are the 33,000 acres of Arches National Monument of which I am now sole inhabitant, usufructuary, observer and custodian.

What are the Arches? From my place in front of the housetrailer I can see several of the hundred or more of them which have been discovered in the park. These are natural arches, holes in the rock, windows in stone, no two alike, as varied in form as in dimension. They range in size from holes just big enough to walk through to openings large enough to contain the dome of the Capitol building in Washington, D.C. Some resemble jug handles or flying buttresses, others natural bridges but with this technical distinction: a natural bridge spans a watercourse—a natural arch does not. The arches were formed through hundreds of thousands of years by the weathering of the huge sandstone walls, or fins, in which they are found. Not the work of a cosmic hand, nor sculptured by sand-bearing winds, as many people prefer to believe, the arches came into being and continue to come into being through the modest wedging action of rain-water, melting snow, frost, and ice, aided by gravity. In color they shade from off-white through buff, pink, brown and red, tones which also change with the time of day and the moods of the light, the weather, the sky.

Standing there, gaping at this monstrous and inhu-man spectacle of rock and cloud and sky and space, I feel a ridiculous greed and possessiveness come over me. I want to know it all, possess it all, embrace the entire scene intimately, deeply, totally, as a man desires a beautiful woman. An insane wish? Perhaps not—at least there's nothing else, no one human, to dispute possession with me.

The snow-covered ground glimmers with a dull blue light, reflecting the sky and the approaching sunrise. Leading away from me the narrow dirt road, an alluring and primitive track into nowhere, meanders down the slope and toward the heart of the labyrinth of naked stone. Near the first group of arches, looming over a bend in the road, is a balanced rock about fifty feet high, mounted on a pedestal of equal height; it looks like a head from Easter Island, a stone god or a petrified ogre.

Like a god, like an ogre? The personification of the natural is exactly the tendency I wish to suppress in myself, to eliminate for good. I am here not only to evade for a while the clamor and filth and confusion of the cultural apparatus but also to confront, immediately and directly if it's possible, the bare bones of existence, the elemental and fundamental, the bedrock which sustains us. I want to be able to look at and into a juniper tree, a piece of quartz, a vulture, a spider, and see it as it is in itself, devoid of all humanly ascribed qualities, anti-Kantian, even the categories of scientific description. To meet God or Medusa face to face, even if it means risking everything human in myself. I dream of a hard and brutal mysticism in which the naked self merges with a nonhuman world and yet somehow survives still intact, individual, separate. Paradox and bedrock.

Well—the sun will be up in a few minutes and I haven't even begun to make coffee. I take more baggage from my pickup, the grub box and cooking gear, go back in the trailer and start breakfast. Simply breathing, in a place like this, arouses the appetite. The orange juice is frozen, the milk slushy with ice. Still chilly enough inside the trailer to turn my breath to vapor. When the first rays of the sun strike the cliffs I fill a mug with steaming coffee and sit in the doorway facing the sunrise, hungry for the warmth.

Suddenly it comes, the flaming globe, blazing on the pinnacles and minarets and balanced rocks, on the canyon walls and through the windows in the sandstone fins. We greet each other, sun and I, across the black void of ninety-three million miles. The snow glitters between us, acres of diamonds almost painful to look at. Within an hour all the snow exposed to the sunlight will be gone and the rock will be damp and steaming. Within minutes, even as I watch, melting snow begins to drip from the branches of a juniper nearby; drops of water streak slowly down the side of the trailerhouse.

I am not alone after all. Three ravens are wheeling near the balanced rock, squawking at each other and at the dawn. I'm sure they're as delighted by the return of the sun as I am and I wish I knew the language. I'd sooner exchange ideas with the birds on earth than learn to carry on intergalactic communications with some obscure race of humanoids on a satellite planet from the world of Betelgeuse. First things first. The ravens cry out in husky voices, blue-black wings flapping against the golden sky. Over my shoulder comes the sizzle and smell of frying bacon.

That's the way it was this morning.

A Natural State

BY STEPHEN HARRIGAN

Except for W. H. Hudson and J.-H. Fabre, Stephen Harrigan is easily my favorite nature writer. One of the main reasons is that he takes nature how and where he finds it—and as he lives in Austin, Texas, he usually finds it in places no one else has ever thought to seek it: puddles that collect beneath clogged drainpipes on disused warehouses, or the high dark places under highway bridges, or the scrawny pine woods that separate a giant water-slide park from a stock-car racetrack twenty miles outside of town. Harrigan wanders everywhere, pokes around, finds amazing things, and has the good sense not to write them off because the places aren't official on the nature map. Instead, he writes them down and offers them to us to read. And we can thank our lucky stars. Not many people can see and think and write like Stephen Harrigan.

In this selection, he sums up—seemingly without the slightest sense of philosophy or favoritism for humans or intellectual superiority—the mystification we have seen so many times from the writers in this book: Where does man fit into all of this orderliness that apparently doesn't need his approval or even attention? And what about me? Where do I fit? Is there anything I can do, or as seems to be the case, is my kind already doing too much?

For Stephen Harrigan, the answer should be easy. Yes, there definitely is something you can do: Keep poking around, keep thinking good-naturedly, and above all, for goodness' sake, keep writing.

When I was six my brother and I used to ride our bikes to a scummy little rainwater pond near our house in Abilene, Texas. The pond was full of old tires and cast-off two-by-fours with protruding nails. Tadpoles gathered in the shallow water near the banks, darting about in a witless frenzy.

Once, my brother, who was a year older, pointed toward a rotting piece of lumber afloat in the middle of the pond and told me there was a water moccasin on it. I'm not sure now if what I saw there was real or imagined; it seems to me that my child's experience of the world was formed as much by hallucination as by reality. The snake might not have been there at all, but

I *remember* it, I see it to this day. It had a strange kind of shape, its body made up of a series of right-angle kinks like those of a stylized serpent on an Aztec temple. We threw rocks at it, but it didn't move. Its eyes were fixed on me, and the more rocks I threw at the snake the more those eyes seemed to hold me in some sort of terrible judgment. Finally its inanimate wrath broke through all my defenses, and I burst into panicked sobs.

I think of that moment as my introduction to nature. I don't know what nature is exactly—whether it is a category that includes human beings or shuts them out—but for me it has always contained that hint of eeriness, the sense that some vital information—common knowledge to all the universe—has been specifically withheld from me. Sometimes, as with the snake, this secrecy has seemed malevolent, but far more often it has been wonderfully tantalizing. For much of my life I have been obsessed with nature, but not in the way a naturalist would be obsessed with it—driven to classify, to define relationships, to comprehend the world's marvelous intricacy. I have simply wanted to feel more fully a part of that intricacy, to see something other than neutral scorn in the eyes of that half-imagined snake.

Reading these essays over again, I'm struck by how consistently that desire is expressed, how again and again their author seems to be pining for something beyond the range of his perception. I wrote these pieces over a period of eight years while on the staff of *Texas Monthly,* and I researched them in the manner of a journalist—through interviews with experts, background reading, and extensive travel. But I've never really felt like a journalist, and I think what drew me to these subjects was the opportunity they offered to hang up the phone and finally just go off somewhere by myself and look and think. While my colleagues at the magazine were working hard to make sense of modern Texas, I found myself drawn to those very things about the state that could never quite be articulated or understood. These essays are as much as anything a record of my own longing, of my search for those vibrant moments in which one can believe that one's existence belongs authentically to the world of nature.

Texas is an imperfect place in which to seek epiphanies about nature. It is a state that still takes pride in its continuing triumph over the land. I suppose I might rather have written about places radiant with uncorrupted natural beauty, where the beaches were not filled with trash and birds did not bathe in road-side oil slicks, where I could have imagined myself as the chronicler of a laboratory-pure wilderness. But I don't come from those places, and it seems to me that a city-bred Texan with an ambivalence about camping and an unsure way with a field guide can be a fair enough witness to a sullied and complicated natural heritage. The Texas landscape is not always beautiful, and in some places, at some moments, it is hardly bearable. But it is resonant and full of secrets, and this book is a tribute to the power with which those secrets are guarded.

IDLE DAYS IN PATAGONIA

BY W. H. HUDSON

Like J.-H. Fabre, W. H. Hudson (my other nominee for Greatest Nature Writer of All Time) is blessed with the sense of how to observe, inquire, experiment, and write. Hudson grew up on a ranch on the pampas of Argentina; from the age of four he had his own horse and lots of time to follow birds to their nests, to watch spiders hunt, to correctly attribute this four-note song to that insect or amphibian or bird. He called himself a "field naturalist" with deprecation, as if his many books (and several scientific papers) were amusements. Instead, he is one of the most honored sources of firsthand natural knowledge that we have, however amusing. His books are masterpieces of flashy intelligence and selfless humility. Certainly he is to birds what Fabre is to insects: our finest observer and most delightful reporter. The novelist Joseph Conrad once named Hudson his favorite "stylist" and, somewhat crankily, said, "The fellow seems to write as the grass grows. And I cannot figure how he does it."

... Bird music, and, indeed, bird sounds generally, are seldom describable. We have no symbols to represent such sounds on paper, hence we are as powerless to convey to another the impression they make on us as we are to describe the odors of flowers. It is hard, perhaps, to convince ourselves of this powerlessness; in my case the saddening knowledge was forced on me in such a way that escape was impossible. No person at a distance from England could have striven harder than I did, by inquiring of those who knew and by reading ornithological works, to get a just idea of the songs of British birds. Yet all my pains were wasted, as I found out afterwards when I heard them, and when almost every song came to me as a surprise. It could not have been otherwise. To name only half a dozen of the lesser British melodists: the little jets of brilliant melody spurted out by the robin; the more sustained lyric of the wren, sharp, yet delicate; the careless half-song half-recitative of the common warbler; the small fragments of dreamy aërial music emitted by the wood wren amidst the high translucent foliage; the hurried, fantastic medley of liquid and grating sounds of the reed warbler; the song, called by some a twitter, of the swallow, in which the quick, upleaping notes seem to dance in the air, to fall more than one at a time on the sense, as if more than one bird sang, spontaneous and glad as the laughter of some fairy-like, unimaginable child—who can give any idea of such sounds as these with such symbols as words! It is easy to say that a song is long or short, varied or monotonous, that a note is sweet, clear, mellow, strong, weak, loud, shrill, sharp, and so on; but from all this we get no idea of the distinctive character of the sound, since these words describe only class, or generic qualities, not the specific and individual. It sometimes seems to help us, in describing a song, to give its feeling, when it strikes us as possessing some human feeling, and call it joyous, glad, plaintive, tender, and so on; but this is, after all, a rough expedient, and, often as not, misleads. Thus, in the case of the nightingale, I had been led by reading to expect to hear a distinctly plaintive song, and found it so far from plaintive that I was swayed to the opposite extreme, and pronounced it (with Coleridge) a glad song. But by-and-by I dismissed this notion as

equally false with the other; the more I listened the
more I admired the purity of sound in some notes, the
exquisite phrasing, the beautiful contrasts; the art was
perfect, but there was no passion in it all—no *human*
feeling. Feeling of some un-human kind there perhaps
was, but not gladness, such as we imagine in the skylark's song, and certainly not sorrow, nor anything
sad. Again, when we listen to a song that all have
agreed to call "tender," we perhaps recognize some
quality that faintly resembles, or affects us like, the
quality of tenderness in human speech or vocal music;
but if we think for a moment, we are convinced that it
is not tenderness, that the effect is not quite the same;
that we have so described it only because we have no
suitable word; that there is really no suggestion of
human feeling in it.

The old method of *spelling* bird notes and sounds
still finds favor with some easy-going naturalists, and
it is possible that those who use it do actually believe
that the printed word represents some avian sound to
the reader, and that those who have never heard the
sound can by this simple means get an idea of it; just
as certain arbitrary marks or signs on a sheet of written music represent human sounds. It is fancy and a
delusion. We have not yet invented any system of

arbitrary signs to represent bird sounds, nor are we likely to invent such a system, because, in the first place, we do not properly know the sounds, and, owing to their number and character, cannot properly know more than a very few of them; and, in the second place, because they are different in each species: and just as our human notation represents solely our human specific sounds, so a notation of one bird's language, that of the skylark, let us say, would not apply to the language of another species, the nightingale, say, on account of the difference in quality and *timbre* of the two.

One cause of the extreme difficulty of describing bird sounds so as to give anything approaching to a correct idea of them, lies in the fact that in most of them, from the loudest—the clanging scream or call that may be heard a distance of two or three miles— to the faintest tinkling or lisping note that might be emitted by a creature no bigger than a fly, there is a certain aërial quality which makes them differ from all other sounds. Doubtless several causes contribute to give them this character. There is the great development of the vocal organ, which makes the voice, albeit finer, more far-reaching than that of other creatures of equal size or larger. The body in birds is less solid; it is filled with air in the bones and feathers, and acts differently as a sounding board; furthermore, the extremely distensible œsophagus, although it has no connection with the trachea, is puffed out with swallowed air when the bird emits its notes, and this air, both when retained and when released, in some way affects the voice. Then, again, the bird sings or calls, as a rule, from a greater elevation, and does not sit squat, like a toad, on his perch, but being lifted above it on his slender legs, the sounds he emits acquire a greater resonance.

There are bird sounds which may be, and often are, likened to other sounds; to bells, to the clanging produced by blows on an anvil, and to various other metallic noises; and to strokes on tightly-drawn metal strings; also to the more or less musical sounds we are able to draw from wood and bone, and from vessels of glass by striking them or drawing the moistened finger-tips along their rims. There are also sounds resembling those that are uttered by mammalians, as bellowings, lowings, bleatings, neighings, barkings, and yelpings. Others simulate the sounds of various musical instruments, and human vocal sounds, as of talking, humming a tune, whistling, laughing, moaning, sneezing, coughing, and so on. But in all these, or in a very large majority, there is an airy resonant quality which tells you, even in a deep wood, in the midst of an unfamiliar fauna, that the new and strange sound is uttered by a bird. The clanging anvil is in the clouds; the tinkling bell is somewhere in the air, suspended on nothing; the invisible human creatures that whistle, and hum airs, and whisper to one another, and clap their hands and laugh, are not bound, like ourselves, to earth, but float hither and thither as they list.

Something of this aërial character is acquired by other sounds, even by the most terrestrial, when heard at a distance in a quiet atmosphere. And some of our finer sounds, as those of the flute and bugle and flageolet, and some others, when heard faintly in the open air, have the airy character of bird notes; with this difference, that they are dim and indistinct to the sense, while the bird's note, although so airy, is of all sounds the most distinct.

THE SIMPLE STORY OF MUSIC

BY CHARLES D. ISAACSON

In this piece, it is nice to see the sounds of nature treated as a kind of rough music, with "music" being reserved for the artificial constructions of human beings with very specific, human-only designs. Too often, some writer tries to pretend a natural sound can be heard as if it were a man-made tune, which is false and kind of patronizing; or another writer will notate natural sounds on the human musical scale, which is pointless and also patronizing; or some composer will borrow a snatch of birdsong or an elephant roar for his clarinet section or his bass trombone, in the middle of a program-music piece, which is okay but superficial. Although Isaacson closes by suggesting that human composers have "set down their interpretations" of nature's vast array of sounds, I don't think he means they set out to do so (with the exception of Olivier Messiaen, who thought birds were God's avatars). I think he means

101

that these "masters" could not help but write music that had already been covered, in a rougher state, by the sea, or the wind, or a forest, or a frog. The interpretation was unconscious, the borrowing unknown; but, thus, all human music is a kind of homage to the larger sounds all around us, which, perhaps, we might start hearing with a bit more acuity and enjoyment.

Music, like flour and iron and all basic things, may be found in a raw, natural state before it is taken by man and perfected, for special consumption, in a multitudinous list of byproducts.

There has yet been found no proper way to mine or fish for music, nor can we go hunting or drilling for it. Though music is found everywhere, the methods of reducing it to final form for the ultimate consumer are not to be compared with the ways of your regular manufacturers. Perhaps some ingenious inventor of the future will find a system of sifting music out of the universal vibrations, or of harnessing the ocean, much as Niagara Falls is now put to work turning out electric power.

For all Nature is a vast musical instrument.

The melodies of birds are marvels of modulation, rhythm and of meaning, especially when expressed to each other in significant phrases.

All active expressions of nature are creating definite harmonies. The gathering storm, finally breaking into a flood, with crashes of thunder and eerie flashes of lightning, is like some great organist in an improvisation on an inspiration.

The sea in all its moods, playful, sparkling, rapturous, treacherous, is creating an infinite number of beautiful compositions.

The running of brooks, the budding of flowers, the stirring of leaves, all are manifestations of music.

Have you ever rested in a deep forest all alone?

There is a noble silence all about you, yet the woods are alive with mysterious melodies. Even when the last note of the last bird has died down, and there is not a breeze stirring, still within the forest there is a pulsing murmur, like a great heart that beats in time. It is the pulse of the forest and of all nature, you are hearing.

Every poet has indited some lines to the music of nature. For instance this quotation from Walt Whitman:

Proud music of the storm!
Blast that careers so free, whistling across the prairie!
Strong hum of forest treetops! Wind of the mountains!
Personified dim shapes, you hidden orchestras,
You undertones of rivers! Roar of pouring cataracts.

Who loves nature, will find himself encountering many representations, here on the shelves of music. Such a list of titles to astonish you! For the masters have set down their interpretations of nature's grander harmonies. You will hear again the birds and the beasts. You will find yourself listening anew to scenes of calm, of storm, of zephyr breezes and curious tornado hurricanes. Again, you will find composers playing you their pictures of the ocean. You will find scenes of all the seasons. There will be many pictures of woods and plains, of desert and mountain, and of starlight, moonlight and sunset.

"THE OWL"
FROM THE BAT POET

BY RANDALL JARRELL

For the next few entries we are entering a world of pure
fiction. But it's still great Nature. What price "Truth"?
This lovely, scary poem is not meant to be attributed to
Mr. Jarrell, a famous twentieth-century poet, though it is
one of the best things he ever wrote. Rather, "The Owl"
is part of a story in which a small brown bat, envious of
the stylish poetry made by the mockingbird in his yard,
attempts to write some verse of his own, unnatural though
it is for a bat to do so. "The Owl" is the bat's first poem.
In the bat's nocturnal world, the predatory owl is the most
fearsome killer, sneaky and smart and immeasurably pow-
erful. Does this menace come across in the bat's poem?
Not bad for a first try, eh?

A shadow is floating through the moonlight.
Its wings don't make a sound.
Its claws are long, its beak is bright.
Its eyes try all the corners of the night.

It calls and calls: all the air swells and heaves
And washes up and down like water.
The ear that listens to the owl believes
In death. The bat beneath the eaves,

The mouse beside the stone are still as death—
The owl's air washes them like water.
The owl goes back and forth inside the night,
And the night holds its breath.

WATERLAND

BY GRAHAM SWIFT

When a writer chooses to have a novel narrated by a particular character in the first person, the author usually chooses a character who has a remarkable gift for putting together a great story. Graham Swift chose such a fellow in the novel Waterland, *and the narrator had the good sense to put first things first. Before getting into the characters who would be peopling the drama, he spent a long time making the reader deeply familiar with the peculiar nature of the story's place on earth: the unique environment known as the Fens. The Fens and its maddening ambivalence between being water and being land, its refusal to be "managed" by dozens of schemes attempted by conquerors of all other land in England, and its quality of quirky incomprehensibility cause the narrator practically to attribute to the Fens a will, an intelligence, a perversity. Clearly, the place is far more important in the book's events than the rolling cast of characters, and the narrator seems justified in his conviction that the Fens deserves the beautifully full and far-reaching description he gives it here.*

The narrator's account includes references to persons, mostly those who had the folly of thinking they could bend the Fens to their own uses. But unlike the presentations of almost every other environment in this book's selection, this essay on the Fens contains no acknowledgment of wildlife. This is because the strange land itself is essentially the wildlife. And the Fens comes across as being as crafty as crows, as dangerous as tigers, as unpredictable as snakes.

We can only be grateful that Graham Swift, who in fact grew up in fen country, picked as his narrator someone who could give us such an intriguing portrait of this beast of an environment. It tells us a lot about this person—but not nearly as much as it tells us about his strange homeland.

About the Fens

Which are a low-lying region of eastern England, over 12,000 square miles in area, bounded to the west by the limestone hills of the Midlands, to the south and east by the chalk hills of Cambridgeshire, Suffolk and Norfolk. To the north, the Fens advance, on a twelve-mile front, to meet the North Sea at the Wash. Or perhaps it is more apt to say that the Wash summons the forces of the North Sea to its aid in a constant bid to recapture its former territory. For the chief fact about the Fens is that they are reclaimed land, land that was once water, and which, even today, is not quite solid.

Once the shallow, shifting waters of the Wash did not stop at Boston and King's Lynn but licked southwards as far as Cambridge, Huntingdon, Peterborough and Bedford. What caused them to retreat? The answer can be given in a single syllable: Silt. The Fens were formed by silt. Silt: a word which when you utter it, letting the air slip thinly between your teeth, invokes a slow, sly, insinuating agency. Silt: which shapes and undermines continents; which demolishes as it builds; which is simultaneous accretion and erosion; neither progress nor decay.

It came first from the coast of Yorkshire and Lincolnshire, borne on the inshore currents which flowed southwards into the ancient Wash. In the blue-black clay which lies under the soil of Cambridgeshire are deposits of silt containing traces of shells of a type occurring on the beaches and cliff-beds of north-east England. Thus the first silts came from the sea. But to these marine silts were added the land silts carried by the rivers, the Ouse, the Cam, the Welland, which drained, and still drain, into the ever-diminishing Wash.

The silt accumulated, salt-marsh plants took hold, then other plants. And with the plants began the formation of peat. And peat is the second vital constituent of the Fens and the source of their remarkable fertility. Once it supported great forests which collapsed and sank when climatic changes caused water to re-immerse the region. Today, it forms the rich, black beet- and potato-bearing soil which is second to none in the country. But without silt, there could have been no peat.

All this was still happening not so long ago. In 870 the Viking fleets sailed with ease as far as Ely, through a region which was still predominantly water. Two hundred years later Hereward, defending the same high ground of Ely, watched his Norman besiegers flounder and drown in the treacherous peat-bogs. The landscape was still largely liquid.

For consider the equivocal operation of silt. Just as it raises the land, drives back the sea and allows peat to mature, so it impedes the flow of rivers, restricts their outfall, renders the newly-formed land constantly liable to flooding and blocks the escape of floodwater. For centuries the Fens were a network of swamps and brackish lagoons. The problem of the Fens has always been the problem of drainage.

What silt began, man continued. Land reclamation. Drainage. But you do not reclaim a land overnight. You do not reclaim a land without difficulty and without ceaseless effort and vigilance. The Fens are still being reclaimed even to this day. Strictly speaking, they are never reclaimed, only being reclaimed. Without the pumps, the dykes and embankments, without the dredging programmes . . . And you do not need to remind a Fenman of the effects of heavy inland rainfall, or of the combination of a spring tide and a strong nor'easter.

So forget, indeed, your revolutions, your turning-points, your grand metamorphoses of history. Consider, instead, the slow and arduous process, the interminable and ambiguous process—the process of human siltation—of land reclamation.

Is it desirable, in the first place, that land should be reclaimed? Not to those who exist by water; not to those who have no need of firm ground beneath their feet. Not to the fishermen, fowlers and reed-cutters who made their sodden homes in those stubborn swamps, took to stilts in time of flood and lived like water-rats. Not to the men who broke down the medieval embankments and if caught were buried alive in the very breach they had made. Not to the men who cut the throats of King Charles's Dutch drainers and threw their bodies into the water they were hired to expel.

I am speaking of my ancestors; of my father's forefathers. Because my name of Crick, which in Charles the First's day was spelt sometimes "Coricke" or "Cricke," can be found (a day's delving into local archives) amongst the lists of those summarily dealt with for sabotaging drainage works. My ancestors were water people. They speared fish and netted ducks. When I was small I possessed a living image of my ancestors in the form of Bill Clay, a shrunken, leathery carcass of a man, whose age was unknown but was never put at less than eighty, a one-time punt-gunner and turf-cutter, who had witnessed in his lifetime the passing of all but the dregs of the old wild fens in our area; who stank, even with his livelihood half gone, of goose fat and fish slime, mud and peat smoke; who wore an otter-skin cap, eel-skin gaiters and whose brain was permanently crazed by the

poppy-head tea he drank to ward off winter agues.
Old Bill lived with his wife Martha in a damp, crack-
walled cottage not far from the Ouse and on the edge
of the shrinking, reed-filled marsh known, after the
watery expanse it had once been, as Wash Fen Mere.
But some said that Martha Clay, who was some
twenty years younger than Bill, was never Bill's wife at
all. Some said that Martha Clay was a witch . . .

But let's keep clear of fairy-tales.

The Dutch came, under their engineer Cornelius
Vermuyden, hired first by King Charles, then by His
Lordship, Francis, Earl of Bedford. Honouring their
employer's name, they cut the Bedford River, and
then the New Bedford River alongside it, to divert
the main strength of the Ouse from its recalcitrant
and sluggish course by Ely, into a straight channel to
the sea. They built the Denver Sluice at the junction
of the northern end of the new river with the old
Ouse, and the Hermitage Sluice at the southern junction. They dug subsidiary cuts, drains, lodes, dykes,
eaus and ditches and converted 95,000 acres into
summer, if not winter, grazing. Practical and forward-
looking people, the Dutch. And my father's fore-
bears opposed them; and two of them were hanged
for it.

Vermuyden left (he should have been rich but the Dutch Wars robbed him of his English fortune) in 1655. And nature, more effectively than my ancestors, began to sabotage his work. Because silt obstructs as it builds; unmakes as it makes. Vermuyden did not foresee that in cutting new courses for the rivers he reduced, not quickened, their flow; since a divided river conducts at any one point a decreased volume of water, and the less water a river conducts the less not only its velocity but also its capacity to scour its channel. The Earl of Bedford's noble waterways gathered mud. Silt collected in the estuaries, where the current of the rivers was no match for the tide, and built up against the sluices.

And Vermuyden did not foresee one other thing. That reclaimed land shrinks—as anything must shrink that has the water squeezed out of it. And peat, above all, which absorbs water like a sponge, shrinks when it dries. The Fens are shrinking. They are still shrinking—and sinking. Land which was above sea-level in Vermuyden's day is now below it. Tens of feet below it. There is no exaggerating the dangers. The invitation to flooding; the diminution of the gradient of the rivers; the pressure on the raised banks; the faster flow of upland water into the deepening lowland basin. All this, and silt.

In the 1690s the Bedford River burst a sixty-foot gap in its banks. In 1713 the Denver Sluice gave way and so great was the silting below it that the water from the Bedford River was forced landwards, upstream, up the old Ouse to Ely, instead of discharging into the sea. Thousands of acres of farmland were submerged. Cottagers waded to their beds.

And at some time in all this, strangely enough, my paternal ancestors threw in their lot with the drainers and land-reclaimers.

Perhaps they had no choice. Perhaps they took their hire where they were forced to. Perhaps they responded, out of the good of their hearts, to the misery of inundated crops and water-logged homes. In 1748, among the records of wages paid to those employed in rebuilding the Denver Sluice, are the names of the brothers James and Samuel Cricke. And in the parish annals of the Crick homeland, which in those days was north of the small town of Gildsey and east of the New Bedford River, are to be found for the next century and a half, and in the same tenacious connection, the names of Cricks. "John Crick: for

repairing the west bank . . ."; "Peter Crick: for scour-
ing the Jackwater Drain and cutting the new Middle
Drain . . ."; "Jacob Crick, to work and maintain the
windmills at Stump Corner . . ."

They ceased to be water people and became land
people; they ceased to fish and fowl and became
plumbers of the land. They joined in the destiny of
the Fens, which was to strive not for but against water.
For a century and a half they dug, drained and pumped
the land between the Bedford River and the Great
Ouse, boots perpetually mud-caked, ignorant of how
their efforts were, little by little, changing the map of
England.

Or perhaps they did not cease to be water people.
Perhaps they became amphibians. Because if you drain
land you are intimately concerned with water; you
have to know its ways. Perhaps at heart they always
knew, in spite of their land-preserving efforts, that
they belonged to the old, prehistoric flood. And so
my father, who kept the lock on the Leem, still caught
eels and leant against the lock-gates at night, staring
into the water—for water and meditation, they say, go
together. And so my father, who was a superstitious
man, always believed that old Bill Clay, the marsh-
man, whose brains were quite cracked, was really,

nonetheless, and if the truth be known, a sort of Wise Man.

When you work with water, you have to know and respect it. When you labour to subdue it, you have to understand that one day it may rise up and turn all your labours to nothing. For what is water, children, which seeks to make all things level, which has no taste or colour of its own, but a liquid form of Nothing? And what are the Fens, which so imitate in their levelness the natural disposition of water, but a landscape which, of all landscapes, most approximates to Nothing? Every Fenman secretly concedes this; every Fenman suffers now and then the illusion that the land he walks over is *not there*, is floating . . . And every Fen-child, who is given picture-books to read in which the sun bounces over mountain tops and the road of life winds through heaps of green cushions, and is taught nursery rhymes in which persons go up and down hills, is apt to demand of its elders: Why are the Fens flat?

To which my father replied, first letting his face take on a wondering and vexed expression and letting his lips form for a moment the shape of an "O": "Why are the Fens flat? So God has a clear view . . ."

TERRA NOSTRA

BY CARLOS FUENTES

Here's an interesting question: After reading a brief passage that involves the natural world in some easily believable manner, could you guess accurately whether you had been in the middle of a novel or a piece of nonfiction?

In some cases (such as in the Italo Calvino selection) the fictitiousness is obvious, and in others it is much less so. We could also say that sometimes the "truthfulness" of certain nonfiction writing is obvious, while at other times it can just as easily seem to be a fantasia. One difference can be that the fiction writer simply seems more assured and aggressive and daring in his command of the language. In this brief selection from Carlos Fuentes's huge novel, we can certainly feel the I-can-do-anything confidence of the brilliant fiction writer, the irrepressible storyteller, the dashing wordsmith. I won't go so far as to say that only a novelist could pull off the bit in here about col-

lapsing men embracing their shadows as they fall in the desert—I would never insult the talent of a nonfiction writer by suggesting limitations on his or her cleverness with metaphor or imagery—but I will say that I certainly felt here as if I were in the grips of a novelist who could take me anywhere.

Oddly enough, despite the worldly realism of this excerpt, Fuentes is known (especially in this novel) for his "magical realism," his willingness to invent and integrate into his story the most fantastic kinds of stuff. We can see that he has the ability to do so.

Almost no one visits this area of the coast. Sun and storm, both equally cruel, dispute this domain. When the heat rules, sea spray sizzles as it splashes upon the hard-crusted earth: no man's foot can bear the heat of the fine black sand that penetrates, and desiccates, the strongest leather breeches. The stream bed dries up like the skin of an ailing hawk, and in its meanders agonize the ruins of ancient shipwrecks. The beach is an oven with neither breeze nor shadow; to walk along it, one must fight the suffocating weight of this sun-drenched terrain. To walk this beach is to wish to escape from it, climb the baking dunes, then mistakenly believe it possible to cross on foot the desert separating the shore from the mountain range.

But the desert is as unmarked as the hands of a cadaver, all lines of destiny wiped clean. Everyone knows the stories of shipwrecked men who have perished here (for only disaster can lead a man to this remote territory), turning in hopeless circles, fighting their own shadows; inveighing against them because they do not rise from the sand; imploring them to float like cool phantoms above their owners' heads; kneeling, finally, to straddle and strangle those implacable ghosts. The brains of the ill-fated melt in this heat, and when that butter-yellow sun no longer rules the coast, the tempest reigns in its stead to complete the task.

COSMICOMICS

BY ITALO CALVINO

A great many fiction writers have turned nature to their non-nature-designed purposes in novels and stories. An environment becomes a "setting" and selected aspects of it may be artificially emphasized to set the background and behavior of a character or a populace, to place limits upon or provide opportunities for certain kinds of action, or to impart a particular atmosphere or context in which the whole story takes place. A murder mystery set in a rain forest is bound to be different from one set in a desert or on an icebreaker ship in the Arctic Ocean. Creatures are picked up or put down by the novelist as well, to serve his plans—a sudden poisonous snake or wandering tiger can be very useful to get rid of a character, for example, or a skittish wild horse that shows a strange willingness to be approached by one particular girl can imply a huge number of things about her inner self and personality. So-called "acts of God"—lightning strikes, tornadoes,

122 • ITALO CALVINO

floods—are used to twist a plot in an instant and cast all characters and action into new pressures. And the scientific likeliness of the event or accuracy of biological details may not really matter all that much to the writer, who can always rightfully say, "Well, after all, it is fiction."

It is far more rare for a writer to do what Italo Calvino does in his story "The Distance of the Moon" in the book Cosmicomics, *from which this excerpt is drawn. With a rather deadpan assurance that seems offhandedly naturalistic if not scientific, the narrator completely invents at least a part of nature all for himself and tells a story set in the laws and the practices they allow, without batting an eye. Simply put, the narrator and his friends have found out that at a certain time and place, the surface of the moon comes close enough to the surface of the earth that a person on a stepladder can grab a flake of moonrock and flip himself neatly up into that body's gravity, and then onto the moon itself. Calvino then describes a few adventures and features of an ordinary frolic on the moon, and then it's time to get down again. Ho-hum, just another day. . . .*

In its way, this is nature writing. It's just that the "nature" is an obvious fabrication. No problem—we're just reading anyway, right? But then perhaps it strikes us: Who really is to say that the equally bizarre but suppos-

edly "real" piece of nonfiction we recently read about Antarctica or the life cycle of the Tasmanian aardwolf is any more the truth, and less a story? Well, maybe the only way to tell is to visit Antarctica or Tasmania or—who knows?—the moon. . . .

. . . All you had to do was row out to it in a boat and, when you were underneath, prop a ladder against her and scramble up.

The spot where the Moon was lowest, as she went by, was off the Zinc Cliffs. We used to go out with those little rowboats they had in those days, round and flat, made of cork. They held quite a few of us: me, Captain Vhd Vhd, his wife, my deaf cousin, and sometimes little Xlthlx—she was twelve or so at that time. On those nights the water was very calm, so silvery it looked like mercury, and the fish in it, violet-colored, unable to resist the Moon's attraction, rose to the surface, all of them, and so did the octopuses and the saffron medusas. There was always a flight of tiny creatures—little crabs, squid, and even some weeds, light and filmy, and coral plants—that broke from the sea and ended up on the Moon, hanging down from that lime-white ceiling, or else they stayed in midair, a phosphorescent swarm we had to drive off, waving banana leaves at them.

This is how we did the job: in the boat we had a ladder: one of us held it, another climbed to the top, and a third, at the oars, rowed until we were right under the Moon; that's why there had to be so many of us (I only mentioned the main ones). The man at the top of the ladder, as the boat approached the Moon, would become scared and start shouting: "Stop! Stop! I'm going to bang my head!" That was the impression you had, seeing her on top of you, immense, and all rough with sharp spikes and jagged, saw-tooth edges. It may be different now, but then the Moon, or rather the bottom, the underbelly of the Moon, the part that passed closest to the Earth and almost scraped it, was covered with a crust of sharp scales. It had come to resemble the belly of a fish, and the smell too, as I recall, if not downright fishy, was faintly similar, like smoked salmon.

In reality, from the top of the ladder, standing erect on the last rung, you could just touch the Moon if you held your arms up. We had taken the measurements carefully (we didn't yet suspect that she was moving away from us); the only thing you had to be very careful about was where you put your hands. I always chose a scale that seemed fast (we climbed up in groups of five or six at a time), then I would cling first with one hand, then with both, and immediately I would feel ladder and boat drifting away from below me, and the motion of the Moon would tear me from the Earth's attraction. Yes, the Moon was so strong that she pulled you up; you realized this the moment you passed from one to the other: you had to swing up abruptly, with a kind of somersault, grabbing the scales, throwing your legs over your head, until your feet were on the Moon's surface. Seen from the Earth, you looked as if you were hanging there with your head down, but for you, it was the normal position, and the only odd thing was that when you raised your eyes you saw the sea above you, glistening, with the boat and the others upside down, hanging like a bunch of grapes from the vine.

. . . Now, you will ask me what in the world we went up on the Moon for; I'll explain it to you. We went to collect the milk, with a big spoon and a bucket. Moon-milk was very thick, like a kind of cream cheese. It formed in the crevices between one scale and the next, through the fermentation of various bodies and substances of terrestrial origin which had flown up from the prairies and forests and lakes, as the Moon sailed over them. It was composed chiefly of vegetal juices, tadpoles, bitumen, lentils, honey, starch crystals, sturgeon eggs, molds, pollens, gelatinous matter, worms, resins, pepper, mineral salts, combustion residue. You had only to dip the spoon under the scales that covered the Moon's scabby terrain, and you brought it out filled with that precious muck. Not in the pure state, obviously; there was a lot of refuse. In the fermentation (which took place as the Moon passed over the expanses of hot air above the deserts) not all the bodies melted; some remained stuck in it: fingernails and cartilage, bolts, sea horses, nuts and peduncles, shards of crockery, fishhooks, at times even a comb. So this paste, after it was collected, had to be refined, filtered. But that wasn't the difficulty: the hard part was transporting it down to the Earth. This is how we did it: we hurled each spoonful into the air with both hands, using the spoon as a catapult. The cheese flew, and if we had thrown it hard enough, it stuck to the ceiling, I mean the surface of the sea. Once there, it floated, and it was easy enough to pull it into the boat. In this operation, too, my deaf cousin displayed a special gift; he had strength and a good aim; with a single, sharp throw, he could send the cheese straight into a bucket we held up to him from the boat. As for me, I occasionally misfired; the contents of the spoon would fail to overcome the Moon's attraction and they would fall back into my eye.

. . . The soil of the Moon was not uniformly scaly, but revealed irregular bare patches of pale, slippery clay. These soft areas inspired the Deaf One to turn somersaults or to fly almost like a bird, as if he wanted to impress his whole body into the Moon's pulp. As he ventured farther in this way, we lost sight of him at one point. On the Moon there were vast areas we had never had any reason or curiosity to explore, and that was where my cousin vanished; I had suspected that all those somersaults and nudges he indulged in before our eyes were only a preparation, a prelude to something secret meant to take place in the hidden zones.

We fell into a special mood on those nights off the Zinc Cliffs: gay, but with a touch of suspense, as if inside our skulls, instead of the brain, we felt a fish, floating, attracted by the Moon. And so we navigated, playing and singing. The Captain's wife played the harp; she had very long arms, silvery as eels on those nights, and armpits as dark and mysterious as sea urchins; and the sound of the harp was sweet and

piercing, so sweet and piercing it was almost unbearable, and we were forced to let out long cries, not so
much to accompany the music as to protect our hearing from it.

Transparent medusas rose to the sea's surface,
throbbed there a moment, then flew off, swaying
toward the Moon. Little Xlthlx amused herself by
catching them in midair, though it wasn't easy. Once,
as she stretched her little arms out to catch one, she
jumped up slightly and was also set free. Thin as she
was, she was an ounce or two short of the weight necessary for the Earth's gravity to overcome the Moon's
attraction and bring her back: so she flew up among
the medusas, suspended over the sea. She took fright,
cried, then laughed and started playing, catching shellfish and minnows as they flew, sticking some into her
mouth and chewing them. We rowed hard, to keep up
with the child: the Moon ran off in her ellipse, drag-
ging that swarm of marine fauna through the sky, and
a train of long, entwined seaweeds, and Xlthlx hanging there in the midst. Her two wispy braids seemed
to be flying on their own, outstretched toward the
Moon; but all the while she kept wriggling and kick-
ing at the air, as if she wanted to fight that influence,
and her socks—she had lost her shoes in the flight—

slipped off her feet and swayed, attracted by the Earth's force. On the ladder, we tried to grab them.

The idea of eating the little animals in the air had been a good one; the more weight Xlthlx gained, the more she sank toward the Earth; in fact, since among those hovering bodies hers was the largest, mollusks and seaweeds and plankton began to gravitate about her, and soon the child was covered with siliceous little shells, chitinous carapaces, and fibers of sea plants. And the farther she vanished into that tangle, the more she was freed of the Moon's influence, until she grazed the surface of the water and sank into the sea.

We rowed quickly, to pull her out and save her: her body had remained magnetized, and we had to work hard to scrape off all the things encrusted on her. Tender corals were wound about her head, and every time we ran the comb through her hair there was a shower of crayfish and sardines; her eyes were sealed shut by limpets clinging to the lids with their suckers; squids' tentacles were coiled around her arms and her neck; and her little dress now seemed woven only of weeds and sponges. We got the worst of it off her, but for weeks afterwards she went on pulling out fins and shells, and her skin, dotted with little diatoms, remained affected forever, looking—to someone who didn't observe her carefully—as if it were faintly dusted with freckles.

This should give you an idea of how the influences of Earth and Moon, practically equal, fought over the space between them. I'll tell you something else: a body that descended to the Earth from the satellite was still charged for a while with lunar force and rejected the attraction of our world. Even I, big and heavy as I was: every time I had been up there, I took a while to get used to the Earth's up and its down, and the others would have to grab my arms and hold me, clinging in a bunch in the swaying boat while I still had my head hanging and my legs stretching up toward the sky.

THE WORLD MY WILDERNESS

BY ROSE MACAULAY

Many of the selections in this book are here because the writers really got it down when they described a particular piece of nature—an unexpected wild place, a peculiar plant, a majestic or secretive creature. We could easily get into the habit of thinking nature is defined by its ultimate inaccessibility, its "otherness."

In this selection, Rose Macaulay turns her curious, alert writer's eye on a couple of creatures appearing before her in a strange environment, with no less dispassionate acumen than any of our other observers would turn on a newly discovered falcon or shark or beetle. It so happens, though, that the creatures are not bugs or birds. They are human beings: two children, a sister and a brother, with whose mother she has been sitting and waiting for them to return up a long old stair from a beach on the Mediterranean Sea. The writer's thoroughness and absolute lack of judgmental attitudes or empathies are a metaphor about how each would fare if faced with a choice between civilization and "the wild"—and are dense and precise and flat. This passage does not quite make us believe that Ms. Macaulay must be one cold-hearted person, but it almost does. But to see only cold appraisal here would be a mistake; Rose Macaulay has simply recognized that even another human is a creature of Nature, one we must take for whatever it is, along with the knowledge that as clearly as we might describe, we can never really "know" someone else inside his or her life any more than we can know the falcon or the beetle.

But now the child arrived, coming up the garden from the path that led down to the shore, Raoul at her heels. She looked childish for her age, small, with bare brown legs, a short pink print frock, draggled and wet, a prawning net trailing from her hand, a colorless, irregular, olive face, full, rather sulky mouth, fine broad forehead, flaggy dark hair, unwaved, perhaps unkempt, flapping about her neck, slanting, secret gray eyes that looked aside, looked often on the ground under a dark, frowning line of brow; something defensive, puzzled, wary about her, like a watchful little animal or savage. The boy, two years younger, had a touch of the same expression; but he looked French, and quick, perhaps clever, nearer to civilization, as if it might one day catch hold of him and keep him, whereas the girl would surely be out of the trap and away, running uncatchable for the dark forest. Raoul too was slight and small, olive and pale; his eyes were large, a clear brown; his features were neater and prettier than Barbary's; as has been mentioned, he looked like his girl mother, who had bored her husband, and her husband's parents, a good deal. His grandmother supposed that the untidy little gamine Barbe led him into much mischief. He too was wet, and smelled of fish.

SILENT SPRING

BY RACHEL CARSON

It is possible that no American book has ever been more influential (radically at first but, after all these years, resolutely) than Rachel Carson's Silent Spring. Before its publication in 1962, books about nature were mostly happy observations full of wonder and beauty, and books this cutthroat-amphetamine-aggressive were dismissed as the very narrow-scoped ravings of crackpots and cranks. Most humans in the developed world thought about the earth one way: The planet was a treasure trove of natural resources that just could not be ruined or exhausted, and the more clever humankind was at figuring out how to use everything it found or invented, the better.

It was possible, for example, for the owners of factories that manufactured ferociously toxic chemicals to believe that dumping their poisonous by-products directly into rivers that flowed through forests and towns would have no effect on the plants, animals, or people who used the water one way or another. It was possible for ranchers in the shoot-'em-up West to decide that one particular critter—the coyote, say, or the corn snake or golden eagle or puma—was a threat to livestock because one such animal had snatched an occasional stray. War was declared on the beast, bounties were offered, and huge shooting parties were dispatched into the hills and plains to kill every cussed one they found, which usually succeeded in greatly reducing the predator's foothold on the local environment. And when smaller, even more rapacious pests—critters the wiped-out big fella used to eat for most of its meals, and thus keep under control—began to multiply crazily and spoil all kinds of things in the business, well, the ranchers refused to see any connection. It was possible for farmers in the Midwest to believe they could spray huge amounts of nasty poisons on the food they were growing to keep the bugs off, without the thought that these poisons might wash down into the soil, leach into local waters, and put some hurt on everyone who drank H_2O or ate fish, from eagles to tourists. Hey, it was possible to believe that putting a chemical that was well known to cause cancer into hot dogs just to make them that nice pink color was a great idea (apparently, we still believe this; check your frankfurter contents label for sodium nitrite).

In short, before Silent Spring, it was possible to

believe that nothing in nature was really all that con-nected to anything else. You could do one thing, and it would have no consequences on another thing. And, by the way, because you were a member of the superior human race, you could do whatever you pleased.

Silent Spring *changed that, made it impossible to be so ignorant anymore. True, you could bitterly hate the book and its message and that message's possible effects on business—but you just couldn't claim those poisons flowing straight out of those pipes into that river just, well, kind of vanished without a trace. Rachel Carson terminated that attitude, just whacked that stupidity. This was nature writing with a knife-edge. It still cuts.*

Elixirs of Death

For the first time in the history of the world, every human being is now subjected to contact with danger-ous chemicals, from the moment of conception until death. In the less than two decades of their use, the synthetic pesticides have been so thoroughly distrib-uted throughout the animate and inanimate world that they occur virtually everywhere. They have been recovered from most of the major river systems and even from streams of ground-water flowing unseen through the earth. Residues of these chemicals linger in soil to which they may have been applied a dozen years before. They have entered and lodged in the bodies of fish, birds, reptiles, and domestic and wild animals so universally that scientists carrying on animal experiments find it almost impossible to locate subjects free from such contamination. They have been found in fish in remote mountain lakes, in earthworms burrowing in soil, in the eggs of birds—and in man himself. For these chemicals are now stored in the bodies of the vast majority of human beings, regardless of age. They occur in the mother's milk, and probably in the tissues of the unborn child.

All this has come about because of the sudden rise and prodigious growth of an industry for the production of man-made or synthetic chemicals with insecticidal properties. This industry is a child of the Second World War. In the course of developing agents of chemical warfare, some of the chemicals created in the laboratory were found to be lethal to insects. The discovery did not come by chance: insects were widely used to test chemicals as agents of death for man.

The result has been a seemingly endless stream of synthetic insecticides. In being man-made—by ingenious laboratory manipulation of the molecules, substituting atoms, altering their arrangement—they differ sharply from the simpler inorganic insecticides of pre-war days. These were derived from naturally occurring minerals and plant products—compounds of arsenic, copper, lead, manganese, zinc, and other minerals, pyrethrum from the dried flowers of chrysanthemums, nicotine sulphate from some of the relatives of tobacco, and rotenone from leguminous plants of the East Indies.

What sets the new synthetic insecticides apart is their enormous biological potency. They have immense power not merely to poison but to enter into the most vital processes of the body and change them in sinister and often deadly ways. Thus, as we shall see, they destroy the very enzymes whose function is to protect the body from harm, they block the oxidation processes from which the body receives its energy, they prevent the normal functioning of various organs, and they may initiate in certain cells the slow and irreversible change that leads to malignancy.

Yet new and more deadly chemicals are added to the list each year and new uses are devised so that contact with these materials has become practically world-wide. The production of synthetic pesticides in the United States soared from 124,259,000 pounds in 1947 to 637,666,000 pounds in 1960—more than a fivefold increase. The wholesale value of these products was well over a quarter of a billion dollars. But in the plans and hopes of the industry this enormous production is only a beginning.

A Who's Who of pesticides is therefore of concern to us all. If we are going to live so intimately with these chemicals—eating and drinking them, taking them into the very marrow of our bones—we had better know something about their nature and their power. . . .

Needless Havoc

As man proceeds towards his announced goal of the conquest of nature, he has written a depressing record of destruction, directed not only against the earth he inhabits but against the life that shares it with him. The history of the recent centuries has its black passages—the slaughter of the buffalo on the western plains, the massacre of the shore-birds by the market gunners, the near-extermination of the egrets for their plumage. Now, to these and others like them, we are adding a new chapter and a new kind of havoc—the direct killing of birds, mammals, fishes, and indeed practically every form of wildlife by chemical insecticides indiscriminately sprayed on the land.

Under the philosophy that now seems to guide our destinies, nothing must get in the way of the man with the spray gun. The incidental victims of his crusade against insects count as nothing; if robins, pheasants, raccoons, cats, or even livestock happen to inhabit the same bit of earth as the target insects and to be hit by the rain of insect-killing poisons no one must protest.

The citizen who wishes to make a fair judgement of the question of wildlife loss is today confronted with a dilemma. On the one hand conservationists and many wildlife biologists assert that the losses have been severe and in some cases even catastrophic. On the other hand the control agencies tend to deny flatly and categorically that such losses have occurred, or that they are of any importance if they have. Which view are we to accept?

. . . The best way to form our own judgement is to look at some of the major control programmes and learn, from observers familiar with the ways of wildlife, and unbiased in favour of chemicals, just what has happened in the wake of a rain of poison falling from the skies into the world of wildlife.

To the bird watcher, the suburbanite who derives joy from birds in his garden, the hunter, the fisherman or the explorer of wild regions, anything that destroys the wildlife of an area for even a single year has deprived him of pleasure to which he has a legitimate right. This is a valid point of view. Even if, as has sometimes happened, some of the birds and mammals and fishes are able to re-establish themselves after a single spraying, a great and real harm has been done.

But such re-establishment is unlikely to happen. Spraying tends to be repetitive, and a single exposure from which the wildlife populations might have a chance to recover is a rarity. What usually results is a poisoned environment, a lethal trap in which not only the resident population succumb but those who come in as migrants as well. The larger the area sprayed the more serious the harm, because no oases of safety remain. Now, in a decade marked by insect-control programmes in which many thousands or even millions of acres are sprayed as a unit, a decade in which private and community spraying has also surged steadily upwards, a record of destruction and death of American wildlife has accumulated.

... Through all these new, imaginative, and creative approaches to the problem of sharing our earth with other creatures there runs a constant theme, the awareness that we are dealing with life—with living populations and all their pressures and counter-pressures, their surges and recessions. Only by taking account of such life forces and by cautiously seeking to guide them into channels favourable to ourselves can we hope to achieve a reasonable accommodation between the insect hordes and ourselves.

The current vogue for poisons has failed utterly to take into account these most fundamental considerations. As crude a weapon as the cave man's club, the chemical barrage has been hurled against the fabric of life—a fabric on the one hand delicate and destructible, on the other miraculously tough and resilient, and capable of striking back in unexpected ways. These extraordinary capacities of life have been ignored by the practitioners of chemical control who have brought to their task no "high-minded orientation," no humility before the vast forces with which they tamper.

The "control of nature" is a phrase conceived in arrogance, born of the Neanderthal age of biology and philosophy, when it was supposed that nature exists for the convenience of man. The concepts and practices of applied entomology for the most part date from that Stone Age of science. It is our alarming misfortune that so primitive a science has armed itself with the most modern and terrible weapons, and that in turning them against the insects it has also turned them against the earth.